# *Mojado*

*R. Allen Chappell*

## Dedication

This book is for Frank Begay, who taught me about his people, and for Jimmy Birdsell, who taught me about my own. May they both now *walk in beauty*.

## Acknowledgments

Again, many sincere thanks to those Navajo friends and classmates who provided "grist for the mill." Their insight into Navajo thought and reservation life helped fuel a life-long interest in their culture, one I had once only observed from the other side of the fence.

Cover art by Labrona & "Other", from the Painted Desert Project on the Navajo reservation.

*Cover design by Terri Chappell.*

*Graphic work by the Kayla Agency*

*Editing by John Baker Limited.*

## Author's note

In the back pages you will find a small glossary of Navajo words and terms used in this story, the spelling of which may vary somewhat, depending on which expert opinion is referenced.

## Table of Contents

The Fix 9
Naked 17
The Gathering 24
The Investigation 34
The Wreck 45
The FBI 55
The Hunt 63
Tressa 71
The Chase 78
The Devil 94
The Cat 102
The Loss 114
The Ingraciado 119
The Witch 123
The Spell 137
Treachery 145
The Twist 151
The Search 166
The Storm 176
Redemption 186
*Glossary* 191

# 1

## *The Fix*

By sundown he had come quite far for one afoot in that country, sun-blistered and worn to the limit of endurance. One arm hung limp from the shoulder and swung useless as he turned to search down canyon. None of these things seemed cause for concern, however. He was from a hard land, accustomed to hard times, and knew no better.

The ragged pants, the tattered shirt unworthy of the name, and the muddy shoes coming apart at the seams—all these things he put in the fire. A fire built with wood he'd found so neatly stacked. He arranged the clothing around the periphery of the flames in such a manner they should cause little smoke and yet be totally consumed. The other clothes (he now considered them his) were draped over a juniper to dry. Everything else he gathered round him, and speculated on the role each might play in the days to come... knowing his life might well depend on them.

~~~~~~

The heifer finally decided something was amiss and allowed herself a moment to ruminate and reflect on the whereabouts of the troublesome little creature. She put her snotty bovine nose in the air and bawled for the calf, listening for the delinquent to come scrambling up the back-trail, where some trifle had diverted his attention. The day was hot and she was loath to turn back down the rocky path in search of that which might appear on its own accord at any moment. It was her first calf, and she was still uncertain what his purpose was. There was, nonetheless, the nagging worry she shouldn't allow him out of sight. True, he'd been nothing but a bother and hindrance throughout their short relationship, but still, there was this thing inside her that demanded she find him.

She had no way of knowing her calf had gotten himself into such a fix, and would not have known what to do about it if she had.

Even before she realized the calf was gone, he was well above his belly in quicksand. Now, nearly up to his muzzle, he had managed to take in a mouthful of the soupy mix, the whites of his eyes showing as he tried to make that little noise which usually attracted the cow, but he could produce no more than a gurgle. *Where was the cow?*

~~~~~~~

By mid-morning, Harley Ponyboy and Thomas Begay were beginning to regret taking the job. They had been on the trail since daylight, leaving the truck and trailer well up the trailhead toward Pastora Peak, and starting their gather horseback at the base of the Carrizos. They had already passed several little bunches of stock but figured to sort those on their way back. This particular young cow, however, was worrisome. She had outpaced the others and seemed determined to quit the country altogether. The sharp clean tracks showed her to be young, and she had a calf. It was almost too late in the year for a calf. That's how first-time heifers are, though—they're the ones you have to watch.

"What the hell you suppose has gotten into her?" Thomas sat sweltering in the heat of a sun already high and hot. "Did Annie mention any of these cows was fresh bought?"

Harley Ponyboy reflected a full minute before answering. "Not that I recall, but this one does seem ta be thinking of home." He grinned. "Home must be somewheres else." Harley knew cows and was well aware they often make up for their lack of intelligence by way of sheer determination. This one seemed to be in that frame of mind. *Bullheaded*, that was the word. It described this cow perfectly, and he could see now how the term came about.

Annie Eagletree's cattle had not been well tended that spring and now were scattered across rather a large area, thanks in part to Annie's second husband, Clyde, whose disinterest in the actual work involved in the cattle business was now becoming apparent. Clyde considered himself more of a gentleman stockman, preferring to spend his time lounging around the sale barn, expounding to his friends on his rising fortunes. He was determined to better himself, he said, and while he admitted it was costing his Annie a good bit of money, he felt she would eventually be well rewarded... and just left it at that.

Annie Eagletree's previous husband had succumbed to radiation poisoning, an affliction not at all uncommon among the reservation's uranium miners. Applicants were often poorly informed regarding the dangers of the occupation, causing a disproportionate number of them to later regret it. Annie's husband had lasted longer than most—long enough to file his claim in the ongoing class action suit against the mining operation. The posthumous settlement had made Annie Eagletree quite well off by reservation standards, and after a proper interlude, she rewarded herself with this dapper little man. He was quite spry for his age and of a gregarious nature. She thought she could eventually make something of him, and had high expectations in that regard. Clyde did, she admitted, drink a bit from time to time, and while she would have preferred someone who didn't, it still was little enough to pay for a man with so many possibilities.

When Charlie Yazzie offered his two friends the job, he made it clear they would be in for a ride. It was rough country and his Aunt Annie's cattle had grown somewhat independent.

Harley Ponyboy's wife, Anita, was said to have flown into a tizzy over Harley taking the day off to gather stock that didn't even belong to them. She thought he might better spend his time working on the roof of their trailer house, which she reminded him leaked like a sieve. She also ventured the opinion that he might be hanging out with Thomas Begay more than was good for him. Harley finally had to remind *her* that it seldom rained in that country and they needed the money *now*. He assured her Charlie Yazzie's aunt was willing and able to pay for his time.

Charlie Yazzie, for his part, said he couldn't afford to take off work to gather cows, nor could he bring himself to take money from his favorite aunt. The truth was, he knew Thomas and Harley were the better trackers and stockmen; he figured they were the men for the job.

Throughout the morning Thomas Begay and Harley Ponyboy continued their dogged pursuit of the fugitive heifer, right up until Thomas halted his piebald gelding at the edge of a wash and spotted something down there in the bottom he didn't like the look of. "Uh-oh," he murmured with a shake of his head.

"What?" Harley Ponyboy scrutinized the wash and almost instantly saw what caught his friend's attention. Only the white head and red back of the bull calf was now visible above the greyish crust. Thomas loosened his catch rope and both men spurred their mounts down the steep talus slope. Thomas, in the lead, had built a loop by the time they reached bottom and pulled his horse up just short of the treacherous bog. Harley's mule, Shorty, had been dubious from the start, and now that he could assess the situation close up was inclined not to participate. He backed up and flattened his long ears in such a manner Harley felt arguing would be unproductive. Shorty had often proven his good sense in such situations; Harley had come to trust his instincts and didn't press the issue.

Most people think quicksand is something found only in swamps or wetlands—certainly not in the high desert Southwest. Truth is, quicksand is not uncommon in the canyon lands. Depressions in the bedrock of canyon floors allow runoff to collect beneath an otherwise benign layer of fine silt. This sort of quicksand is often the more dangerous due to drying of the top layer, causing it to look like any other patch of sand. It is something even the savvy tourist has learned to look out for.

Thomas indicated the calf with his chin. "I'll see if I can drop a loop on him and keep his head up... I don't want to break his neck trying to jerk him out, though." He grinned. "Looks like one of us is going to have to get in there and help."

"One of us...?" Harley frowned. "Meaning me, I guess...?" But he was already out of the saddle and testing the edge of the quagmire. Harley was not one to shirk his part in an enterprise once committed, and Thomas was already holding the rope and ready to throw.

Shorty snorted and drew back another step.

"That shelf of slick rock runs just underneath this mess... I don' think it's too deep." Harley said this last part with a measure of doubt but pulled off his boots and, holding on to Thomas's rope, moved slowly out toward the calf. The calf didn't like the look of Harley Ponyboy and began thrashing its head, covering his rescuer with muck.

Thomas backed his own horse up a foot or so, re-dallied the rope around the horn, and began shouting advice. "Reach down in there and grab a hind leg, Harley! Maybe we can ease him out of there without me having to pull his head off."

Nearly halfway to the calf, Harley paused to wipe the mud from one eye, glared back at Thomas Begay, and then studied where a hind leg might be in that morass. "Right," he yelled back, "I'll just reach down in there, grab a leg, and pitch him out ta you! You be careful, now, I don't hit you with him... Nuthead!" The two had been friends a long time and neither was shy about telling the other what he thought. Harley was now in well above his knees and having a hard time pulling his own feet loose. He stayed clear of the calf's flailing head. It was a Hereford, a good stout little fellow, capable of knocking him right off his feet should it get lucky. That might put *him* in line to be rescued as well—it's not easy to regain lost footing in quicksand.

Thomas Begay spoke calmly to his horse and cautiously climbed down, leaving the nervous gelding to keep the rope taut. He had spent a lot of time schooling this horse in the rudiments of calf roping and hoped now it would pay off.

"Watcha' do'n, Thomas? I don' think that horse has sense enough ta hold a calf without you on him." Harley remembered Thomas's horse as being a little dicey when the chips were down.

"This horse will be fine. I been working with him; he'll hold him all right." Thomas spoke in a quiet, measured tone but watched the horse's eyes—he would see it there first should the gelding decide his heart wasn't in it. He inched over to Harley's saddle, took the rope off, and moving up to the edge, threw it out to him. "If you can get this loop under his tail, I'll try to pull as you lift—it might work."

Harley cocked an eye at Thomas. "Might work?" he mumbled to himself as he reached down through the slime, feeling for the calf's hind leg, which caused the calf to struggle even harder. "I think I got it," he yelled, and gave a mighty heave.

Thomas stared with rounded eyes at the sight of the blue-grey hand and arm being pulled from the mire—the thin pale hand of someone not long dead. "You better get out of there, Harley." Thomas could barely choke out the words.

Harley froze, eyes riveted on the claw-like hand. Every fiber of his being screamed for him to flee, but that was obviously not an option. He spoke softly then, "Let's get this calf out; the other can wait," and after a moment's thought, "It's a white man... I don' think white people have a *chindi*." Harley came from very traditional people, and the Navajo fear of the dead was deeply ingrained, but he was a pragmatist as well and knew there was nothing for it now but to carry on and try not to think of what lay below the roiled surface.

Once the calf was on solid ground, it stood spraddle-legged and shaking. Blowing mud and snot from its nostrils, it looked suspiciously back at Harley still in the bog, then struggled to make some sort of sound. Thomas quickly released both ropes and pitched the lines back out to Harley who, after securing one around his own chest, again reached into the cold grey muck for the abandoned remains of whoever was down there.

When he clambered out, wiping mud from his face, and catching his breath, he was finally able to speak. "That other rope is tied ta his arm. I think he's fresh enough to pull him out in one piece if we take it slow and easy."

Thomas looked cautiously at the hand still sticking out of the quicksand. "I have a better idea. Let's not mess with him. I say we just tie this end of the rope to that little cedar tree. That should make it easy for someone to locate him later, and he won't migrate any further downstream." He glanced up at the ridge. "It's too far back in here to try and pack him out. The authorities can be back in by chopper before we could get him out anyway." Thomas was not so traditional a Navajo as Harley but was just as afraid of the dead and the possibility of the evil spirits that most often come attached. *Chindi* are universally evil and known to be capable of all manner of bad things, should they hook onto a person.

Offered this easier option, Harley Ponyboy instantly agreed. "I expect you're right," he conceded, then pursed his lips toward the dead person. "Anyhow, he'll probably keep better down there in the cold than across a horse in this heat." Harley scoured a dry lump of mud off the back of his neck and then, almost as an afterthought, said, "That guy out there is naked."

Thomas narrowed an eye at Harley. "What makes you think he's naked?"

Harley Ponyboy just grimaced, shrugged, and looked away. "He's naked."

Behind them they heard a scrambling and scattering of shale as the fugitive cow chose that moment to come skidding down the embankment, throwing her head from side to side and clearly on the fight. She lowered her horns and slung slobber as she pawed the ground, trying to decide which of the interlopers would be first to pay. Fortunately, the calf, happy to see the cow at last, defused the situation by wobbling over to the heifer and nudging her bag, caused her to let down her milk... everything was again right in their world.

## 2

*Naked*

Legal Services investigator Charlie Yazzie looked across his corner of the office, saw Thomas Begay at the reception counter, and signaled the Bitter Water Clan woman to allow him to pass. Thomas was of the Bitter Water Clan himself, but apparently the woman didn't recognize him—there were a lot of Bitter Water people in that country, and it was hard to tell just by looking.

Charlie kicked out the chair across from his desk and sat back to hear his friend's version of what had happened the day before. When Thomas had called him from Annie Eagle-tree's new telephone, he first thought it was one of his never-ending practical jokes—several minutes were required to clear that up. Charlie was in it then and spent the rest of the day and part of the following morning with the various legal authorities involved in the gruesome discovery.

"So, what's the word from the feds?" Thomas knew tribal police would have been first to be notified, but in the end it would come down to the FBI. Though the Navajo Nation had become more autonomous over the years, the government still liked to keep a finger in the pie, so to speak. The FBI, along with the Bureau of Indian Affairs, continued to wield rather big sticks on the reservation.

"So far, not much from the agent in charge. He's the new guy that took Davis's place. I haven't even met him yet." Charlie chose his words carefully and lowered his voice, keeping an eye on the receptionist, who was known to gossip. "It will be a few days before their lab issues its findings, but the preliminary says there was water in the lungs and the body was pretty well battered. Death may have been from drowning... or it could have been from the other injuries, apparently. However, they didn't think those other injuries were particularly life threatening." He paused to let Thomas ponder the possibilities while he sifted through papers on his desk, looking for the fax he'd received from the tribal boys that morning.

"Harley thought the guy was naked," Thomas interjected, wrinkling his nose slightly at the very thought. "Anything in there about that?" He still couldn't believe what Harley had done. "He's out right now looking for someone to do a cleansing ceremony. I told him to go see my father-in-law, old man Paul T'Sosi. *He* can do that cleansing ceremony as good as anyone, and he won't charge Harley an arm and a leg either... he likes Harley."

Charlie nodded as he continued to study the report. "Harley was right. The guy was naked," he went on reading from the paper, "White male, about thirty-five years old, no real identifying marks on the body, and a near-perfect set of teeth." He flipped the paper over and reread a note from tribal police officer Samuel Shorthair, a longtime acquaintance and probably the only reason he had received anything in the first place. "You remember Sam Shorthair?"

"I remember he was two years ahead of us in school and was one of the dorm monitors who was on my ass all the time." Thomas had been somewhat of a case in school, and were it not for his abilities on the football field, might not have lasted out his final year of government boarding school, at least not without some serious repercussions. Thomas's coach had taken a liking to him, and thinking the boy had potential, often ran interference for him with other white teachers. Things might otherwise have ended badly for Thomas.

"Yeah, well anyway, Sam left me a note on the back of this fax saying they found a camp, just up the canyon from where the body was recovered. Just a small backpacking tent, apparently. There was no clothing, pack, food, or sleeping bag… just the tent." Charlie ran a finger along the words, then stopped. "Oh, and the dead guy's fingernails were worn to the quick… right into the finger tips."

When Charlie looked up, Thomas Begay had rocked back in his chair, eyes nearly closed. Charlie thought for a moment he might have dozed off. Thomas was known to catch a nap when he could. But then his eyes blinked open, and bringing his chair upright he fixed Charlie with a look. "Were they able to get his prints?"

"I don't know." Charlie glanced again at the paper. "It doesn't say. Sam says he will get back to me, if and when he finds out any more. The FBI generally sends tribal police follow-up reports in this sort of case, but they seldom include anything of any real value. They keep the good stuff to themselves."

"Do you think it would do any good if *we* took a run back up there for a look around… maybe take Harley with us. He's a hell of a tracker when he's sober, which he has been for a good while." Thomas added this last part to assure Charlie of their friend's continued good intentions. Harley's recent fall from grace had been a disappointment to them both, but especially to Thomas, who well knew what Harley had gone through to quit, and how easy it would be for him to fall off the wagon himself. He had known any number of people who swore off drinking for various lengths of time— many for three or four or even six months… or a year even– –then, bam! They were off and running again. It was a reservation phenomenon that had, over the years, become part of the culture; it was hard to say where in the cycle any one person might be at any particular time.

When appearing before a federal commission, New Mexico's Alcohol Beverage Control Director once said, "Alcoholism is destroying the Navajo Nation, and the situation is a national disgrace, if not a national disaster." Thomas grimaced when he remembered how long ago the report had been made... years ago; but little had come of it. The problem was still endemic. He also knew he might well have returned to drink himself had it not been for his two children coming back into his life; they had no one else to turn to now, and he knew it. He thought it a pitiful state of affairs that nearly sixty-five percent of the Navajo Nation, at some point in their lives, are said to find alcohol abuse a problem. The government acknowledges the affliction as the leading cause of life-threatening medical complications and death throughout the reservation... not to mention, eighty percent of reservation crime can be attributed to it. Even Charlie admitted he could see no solution to the problem in the foreseeable future.

Charlie Yazzie twirled a pencil back and forth between two fingers. "I doubt we could do any good up there after the place has been mucked up by everyone else," he said referring to Thomas's previous question. "Probably looked like Grand Central Station, what with the recovery effort and all."

Thomas knew Grand Central Station was a train station, and just figured Charlie meant there'd be a lot of tracks. He didn't always get what Charlie meant when he alluded to things and places he himself had no experience with.

Charlie pursued his previous train of thought. "I'll think about it." He kicked Thomas's chair under the table. "Hey, you know tomorrow's Saturday; there's the barbeque up at our place?"

"Yep, Lucy told me. Old Man Paul T'Sosi says he's coming too, which is good. He can help keep an eye on the kids, and I know he's looking forward to giving a little prayer at the baby's naming. He's been feeling better lately, but we still don't like to leave him home by himself." Thomas looked down at his boots. "I don't know what it is about that old man...I'm sure he doesn't like me... never has, but still I'd hate to see anything happen to him." He looked away for a moment before going on, "Harley and Anita will be there, too, at least according to Harley." He examined a fresh rope burn on his throwing hand and frowned. "You know, Anita never comes to *our* get-togethers. I guess she still thinks I'm a bad influence on Harley, or something. She doesn't seem to remember that *he* was the last one to get his ass in trouble drinking, not me."

Charlie only nodded. Thomas Begay and Harley Pony-boy had been drinking buddies for years and finally had quit the bottle about the same time. Harley had fallen off the wagon for a short time the previous year but had made a valiant turnaround. Thomas himself had been sober almost two years now, but still had a hard time dealing with his past and the consequences he had brought upon himself. Charlie knew his friend was always only one drink away from square one. It wasn't easy being Thomas.

~~~~~~~~

In the pre-dawn chill, the *mojado* threw off his recently acquired sleeping bag—he had not known there were such wonderful things and had almost left it behind. He realized now that each piece of this equipment had a carefully thought out purpose. He had done well to take the trouble to get these things. It had not been so much trouble really, and while it had cost one man his life, it had probably saved that of another—that's the way he looked at it. If he'd had the use of both arms, it would have been easier yet. He had left behind only the tent, a silly little thing to his way of thinking, but he *had* taken its plastic ground cloth, just in case. He didn't quite know what to make of the freeze-dried food (there was a lot of it), but he thought it might prove to be quite a windfall once he understood its preparation; pictures on the foil packets gave clues to what each pouch contained, and he was confident he would figure out the process in time. For now, though, he just tore open the package with a picture of some little brown cakes... He hoped they would be chocolate, and they were. He ate these as he re-stuffed the down sleeping bag, marveling once again at its feathery weight.

As he moved out in the graying dawn, he fingered the hefty Buck knife folded in his pocket and thought what a prize it would be back home. Where he came from, a man without a knife was no man at all. A knife like this could make all the difference, and down the road, he expected it had its work cut out for it.

~~~~~~~

Charlie Yazzie picked up the incoming fax and leafed through the copy of the latest FBI "update" from Sam Shorthair. A scrawled note on the front from Sam warned him not to expect any earth shattering developments. Reading between the lines of an FBI case report prepared for other agencies was always an exercise in futility. The FBI had played their cards close to the vest since the days of Herbert Hoover, when they had actually worn vests. They'd learned back then the value of keeping things to themselves. Nonetheless, Charlie still caught himself trying to read more into this report than was actually there. The update included the usual generic information, things anyone might later pick up from reading the newspaper, or listening to a radio. But, there was also a smattering of tidbits they thought might placate the various agencies, without letting any cats out of the bag, as his grandmother had been fond of saying. The FBI felt they had the best investigative techniques, the latest technology and facilities, and therefore just assumed they must also have the brightest people. Generally speaking, they were right on all counts and thus were reluctant to let lesser entities screw things up. It was an elitist policy that left the rest of the agencies muddling along in the wake of an organization they considered to have... an attitude. The few bones the bureau threw "tribal" always had the meat gnawed off, in Charlie's opinion. Still, he knew tribal police would dogged-ly work their investigation regardless of how little they actually had to go on. There *were* a few scraps in this last update, and Charlie Yazzie intended to make the most of that information.

# 3

## *The Gathering*

Saturday morning saw Charlie Yazzie's wife excited and up early to begin preparations for the feed they were putting on for close friends and family. "Some of these people," Sue declared, "are coming a long way and deserve the best we can come up with." She herself would be making two large chocolate cakes, which she had recently learned how to bake in her new oven. The first few cakes had "fallen" when taken out to cool, making them look a little lopsided. Sue just added extra icing and no one seemed the wiser. Everyone liked icing the best anyway. These particular two cakes looked perfect, and she was anxious to see how they went over. Aunt Annie Eagletree was sometimes critical when it came to Sue's cooking, and not shy about venturing an opinion... and she didn't care who overheard it either.

There would also be fresh corn from her own garden, soaked in cold water, then steamed in the husk in hot ashes. It had been her people's preferred method of cooking green corn for over a thousand years now, and was still hard to improve on. Other women would be bringing covered dishes, and Aunt Annie Eagletree insisted on bringing a front quarter of beef they had butchered only the day before. Her husband Clyde had taken the animal to the locker plant in Farmington so it could be professionally done. Annie thought it an unnecessary expense, as she had always done her own butchering right at home. This allowed her the exact cuts of meat she preferred she said, something the locker plant might not understand how to do. She did tell Clyde to make sure they got back the kidneys and tongue, along with the neck bones and even the tail, as she had heard those people at the facility sometimes kept those things, along with the hide, as part of their fee. Those were all good parts and shouldn't go to waste or into dog food, as she had been warned could happen; cowhides came in handy for a lot of things as well, and she didn't intend to let this one go, even if it did cost a little extra to keep it.

Lucy Tallwoman told her husband, Thomas, she intended to bring a considerable amount of fry-bread dough, already mixed and ready to pat out and drop in the hot oil. Fry-bead had to be eaten freshly cooked to be right she said. She also made a succotash of corn, beans, and squash, just as the Diné had done since they came into that country. Her grandmother had said the dish was given them in ancient times by their Pueblo neighbors, who she guessed had invented it. Thomas Begay would stop in town for ice to fill Sue's washtub, already packed with sodas and bottles of water.

This was to be the official naming day for Charlie and Sue's son, who was already toddling about and getting in the way of the flurry of preparations in his honor. Only family and close friends knew his Navajo name: *Ashkii Ana 'Dlohi* or Laughing Boy. That was from a book Charlie had read at university. Navajo children often have their pet names changed as they grow, usually marking a single memorable incident or happening in their lives. Sometimes one of these names will stick—not always a happy thing for the child. Sue had a cousin who still carried his childhood name of "Mudhead," which his brothers' thought fit him at the time. Sue's son had already gone by several names, and there would be others as time went on. Today, however, his real "birth certificate" name would be made known—the name listed on the tribal rolls, and the one that would identify him for all time as a member of the Navajo Nation: Wiley Joseph Yazzie. Sue had first suggested it, saying she had got the idea from a movie, and Charlie, after thinking it over, thought it good enough. Joseph had been his grandfather's name, and he wished his grandmother had lasted long enough to hear it.

When everyone arrived, the men went around shaking hands (as Navajos are prone to do at the slightest opportunity) and talking while they had a soda, as the women got busy with the food. Harley Ponyboy and his wife Anita arrived last, bringing a pot of pinto beans and a huge container of her specialty—green chili with pork. Lucy Tallwoman's father, Old Man Paul T'Sosi, teamed up with Aunt Annie's Husband, Clyde, to man the grills and start the various cuts of meat sizzling. Clyde had brought a pint of fairly good whiskey in his meat cooler and from time to time he and Paul T'Sosi would have a little nip when they thought no one was looking.

Thomas's uncle, John Nez, had been invited along with his white live-in girlfriend, Marissa, who was now considered his new wife by most people up near Navajo Mountain, where John Nez had recently been elected to the tribal council. No one up there thought the less of him for "marrying" a white woman. It had turned out to be a mutually beneficial arrangement as it provided anthropologist Marissa an "in" that might only be dreamed about by less fortunate students of the culture. There were more than a few whites living on the reservation, some as spouses of Indians, and it no longer carried the stigma it once had. Still, secretly, each culture looked askance at the practice and didn't quite know what to make of it.

Charlie Yazzie, along with Thomas Begay and Harley Ponyboy, gravitated to the far side of the gathering and immediately fell to talking about the grisly discovery up at Pastora Peak.

Harley, living farther away from town and without a driver's license or telephone, had not been kept in the loop as far as the latest information went, and since it was his find in the first place, felt somewhat slighted, and said as much. "So... what? No one could drop by our place and let me know what's going on?"

Charlie looked up and shook his head. "It's a long way out there, Harley. We've had a lot going on."

Thomas elbowed Harley in the ribs and laughed. "You should move closer to town, *hostiin*. If you want, I'll hook onto that old trailer of yours and pull it up here in Charlie's backyard." Thomas was inordinately proud of his diesel truck and missed no opportunity to advertise its pulling capability. "The salesman said it would pull a house off its foundation," he assured them for the second or third time.

Charlie motioned his friends over to the corrals and glanced back at the crowd. "We got another update from the feds."

Thomas perked up his ears and moved closer. "About time."

Charlie hesitated only a moment before deciding these two should be kept fully abreast of developments since they were already a part of the case, and he knew they would keep things to themselves. He lowered his voice and went over the latest information.

There was a positive identification of the victim, who proved to be a recent graduate and academic from UNM's archaeology department named R. J. Tyler, apparently out on a little personal field trip. He'd not seen fit to obtain the requisite tribal permits, however, so his wife had dropped him off at a trailhead southeast of Teec Nos Pos, only three days before the discovery of his body. She *was* to have picked him up seven days later at a more distant trailhead farther down country. She told federal agents her husband was well credentialed and an experienced backcountry trekker. What she could not seem to tell them was why he had not secured the required paperwork. The Navajo Nation requires permits for backcountry exploration by outsiders, and especially where concentrations of archaeological sites are involved, permits might even involve a mandatory Navajo guide. The lack of permits in this instance was probably the reason the grad student had his wife drop him off, instead of making his presence known by leaving a vehicle at a trailhead. This was not an uncommon dodge among some backpackers—an independent lot—who, for the most part, don't care to be on a tether. The Navajo Nation, in its defense, cites an increasing number of people who insist on getting lost each season—sorely taxing tribal resources. Of course, Charlie also knew the guide requirements added a badly needed income stream for the tribe, and that probably had something to do with the edict. Navajo guides do not come cheap.

Then too, there was always the possibility that a local resident would accost a likely stranger, and demand he buy an additional permit for crossing their "private" land. This "permit" was often more costly than the official one. It was better, some visitors thought, to just pay if you got caught and avoid the double jeopardy.

As Charlie reviewed the previous day's fax, the only real evidence of foul play was the fact that all the man's possessions were missing except his tent. Odd, Charlie thought, it was an expensive tent, light and compact, designed for quick and easy portability. Either someone didn't know the value of such a thing, or perhaps already had one and didn't want to bother packing off another. Contrary to popular conception, today's Indians, aside from the occasional herder, seldom see the inside of a tent and couldn't care less. Most of the traditional Navajo's life is spent virtually "camping out" anyway. Camping as a recreational pursuit remains somewhat foreign to most.

Charlie took a deep breath and went on, "Foul play can't be ruled out, but based on the current evidence, the death might well have been caused by a fall or other accident." He looked at the other two. "Don't you think it's possible it was accidental and some passerby pilfered the deceased's belongings after the fact?" This seemed the most likely scenario to Charlie's way of thinking. This, of course, left several niggling little questions: Why was the man naked? Why would someone take his clothing? "According to his wife's description, her husband's clothes had been well worn—including his hiking boots—not worth taking for the average person." *It could have been someone in dire need,* he thought to himself, *and there are people around there who fit that description, but even this seems unlikely in view of the isolated area involved, and one with so few inhabitants.*

Thomas looked up and across the pasture as though searching the cottonwood trees along the irrigation ditch for an answer. "I still say we take another little ride up there and have a look-see for ourselves." He shot Charlie a searching glance and said, "Something doesn't add up."

Harley agreed. "I go along with that. Those FBIs might be pretty smart and all, but I wonder if they even cut any circles looking for sign. Those young tribal policemens can't read sign neither. No one takes the time ta learn that stuff anymore." Harley, by virtue of his recent cleansing ceremony, was now invested in the case and felt some intangible need to contribute to a satisfactory conclusion.

Charlie sighed. "Well, tomorrow is Sunday. I guess we could take a little run up there and see if anything jumps out at us."

"Don' say 'Jumps out at us.' That dead person's *chindi* could still be hanging around up there." Harley was now having second thoughts.

"Whoa!" Thomas didn't like the sound of it either. He glared at Harley. "I thought you said white people didn't have *chindi*?"

"Well, my father always said they didn't, but what the hell did he know? He never saw no dead white person that I know of, and neither did I, before this." Harley frowned. "Who knows what white peoples have got. They must have some kind of spirit inside them," and after thinking a moment added, "but maybe not mean ones like our *chindi*."

Charlie turned back to the barbeque. "I don't think *chindi* will be a problem." Charlie chose not to believe in many of the old ways, and while he didn't disparage them to his friends, his years away at boarding school and then university had caused him to become somewhat ambivalent when it came to traditional myths and religion. Why, even old Paul T'Sosi occasionally interspersed his blessings with a little Christian embellishment, which came, Charlie surmised, from his long years as a handyman for the local Episcopal mission. The Navajo have always adopted what they like from other cultures as long as it made sense to them and didn't impinge too heavily on the bedrock of their own beliefs.

That reminded Charlie, and he eyed Harley Ponyboy. "How did that cleansing ceremony with Paul T'Sosi go? Do you feel better now?" Charlie had an honest interest in the thing but suspected most of the good coming from these ceremonies was psychological at best. But since he considered the malady itself to be psychological, he supposed it might make sense that it worked... once a person thought about it.

Harley tried to remember how he felt about the cleansing and how it might have helped him. Thomas had taken part in it as well, and each had later agreed it took a weight off their mind. It had taken only an hour to put the whole thing together. A few long branches planted in the ground, tied together at the top, and covered with heavy blankets sufficed for the sweat lodge, and the round stones for a fire-ring were borrowed from the border of Lucy Tallwoman's garden. There was plenty of dry cedar wood on hand, and before he knew it, Harley was naked, in the dark, and dribbling water over white-hot rocks. Occasionally a cleansing rite ended badly when too much cold water was dumped on the rocks, causing one of them to explode and injure the patient, in which case the treatment became worse than the affliction. He had also known of several scalding incidents suffered from the live steam. Harley took special pains not to make these mistakes.

Old Man Paul T'Sosi, just outside the sweat lodge, chanted the prayers and Harley joined in on the parts he knew, trusting to the old man to make up any difference. Since it was Harley that had actually touched the body (and he was paying cash money) more attention was paid to his ceremony, and Paul endeavored to make sure everything went exactly as it should.

Thomas's purification was shorter and lacked some of the enthusiasm of Harley's. Thomas suspected it was because he didn't pay anything—his father-in-law doing the ceremony more as a family obligation… and to eliminate any evil from hanging around the family digs.

Harley finally answered Charlie's question. "Well, I feel better about the whole thing now. I don't have that little fear in me anymore, and it didn't cost much neither, so it was good insurance, I guess."

After everyone at the barbeque had eaten, they gathered round and Charlie held his son high for everyone to see. Paul T'Sosi gave a short blessing, much as he had for the boy's initial "Indian name" ceremony, and again offered blue corn pollen to the four sacred mountains. Only then was Charlie and Sue's son formally introduced to his official name. Sue had tried to adhere to the old ways from the beginning, right down to burying a portion of the infant's umbilical cord in the corrals. She thought it somehow important the boy should be exposed to as much *Diné* culture as possible in his early years. Later, when he was older, he could decide for himself how much he needed to take from the traditional ways. His new name would not likely get much use, at least until he started school—most of those present preferred his Navajo name, even when it was spoken in English.

Everyone brought some little something as a gift for the boy on this special day. Old Man Paul T'Sosi gave a tiny flint bird point he had found near an Anasazi cliff dwelling when he himself was a boy. He thought many of those little arrowheads had themselves been gifts to young boys back in that time, and figured it might help this child as well. It would be placed in the small beaded medicine bag he had previously brought the boy on the day the child had been given his Indian name months before. Paul had already given Thomas's son, Caleb, a similar small bag to be carried around his neck, and had passed along his only other bird point to his adopted grandson. Both of those relics were from *his* own medicine bundle or *jish*. The old man knew it would not be long before he himself would no longer need them.

John Nez and his partner Marissa took their obligation in this gift giving quite seriously and had thought long and hard on an appropriate gift. It was Marissa's idea to bring the boy a brilliant red headband and matching sash just as the old Navajo leader Narbona was said to have once worn.

Others had brought similar items of a traditional nature, and soon there was a small pile of such things as a hand-woven saddle blanket by Lucy Tallwoman and a thin silver bracelet Thomas had made the boy. Aunt Annie Eagletree had a small but expensive turquoise belt buckle, made by a Zuni craftsman just for the boy, and though he probably wouldn't be wearing it for a while, it was oohed and aahed over by the entire group. When the party broke up at sun-down, everyone went away with portions of the beef quarter that was left uncooked and as much of the other food as they cared to take home with them. That was the Navajo way and showed proper respect; the hosts would have been quite disappointed if it had not happened just so.

Little Wiley Joseph Yazzie was paraded around the circle one last time to show off his new finery and was already fast asleep by the time Sue put him in his bed.

# 4

## *The Investigation*

The next day on the drive up to the Carrizos, Thomas Begay again speculated on the happenings that ended the life of R. J. Tyler. "I been thinking about this, and there's still a couple of things we haven't chewed over."

Harley Ponyboy grunted, "I don' need to talk about it no more."

Charlie ignored Harley's remark and looked across at Thomas. "What's that?"

"Well, for one thing, what was up with the guy's fingers being torn up at the ends? How do you figure that?"

"Maybe a coyote chewed them off," Harley offered from the rear seat. "I've heard they will eat a person's fingers and toes if they get a chance."

In the old days very young children were often told stories like these to keep them in line and close by the camp. The other two men suspected this was what Harley's comment was based on and smiled remembering many similar stories from their own childhood, and there was little doubt in anyone's mind that such things were possible.

The horseback ride up the side canyon at the base of Pastora Peak went more quickly this time, and the three passed the stretch with pointed suppositions back and forth of what might have happened to the young archaeologist, R. J. Tyler, and pondered his untimely end.

Charlie's gelding ultimately took the lead, as he was well rested and eager to go. Charlie still thought a lot of the horse and disregarded the fact that his previous owner had been the notorious Ute malcontent, Hiram Buck.

"A really good horse, like an exceptional dog, might come along only once in a man's life," Charlie opined. This caused the men's conversation to turn to horses, and Thomas Begay said he had known some who claimed having had two or even three good horses. But, as with women, this would be a rare thing in his view.

As Harley rode a mule, he stayed out of the talk of horses altogether but still felt his Shorty the superior animal.

On the subject of dogs, when it came up, Charlie declared his intention to get his son a pup in the near future and hoped it would be one the boy would always remember. To his mind it was best a boy have a pup as early as possible. At the barbeque, old Paul T'Sosi had mentioned his neighbor's bitch had pups by *his* dog, which, though it had no name, and was only called "dog," was known to be a good one. His son would be lucky to have a dog as fine as Paul's. They, of course, had no sheep to herd, but to his way of thinking there was more to it than that. *There is a lot a dog can teach a boy, more even than the boy might teach the dog.* He remembered his own dog, a scruffy black and white Navajo dog that had twice warned him of a rattlesnake when herding his grandmother's sheep. That dog had died of poison when the government decided to eradicate a prairie dog town during an outbreak of Hanta virus. Later it was said the virus was mostly just carried by mice and kangaroo rats in their particular area, but it was too late for the prairie dogs... and his own dog too.

When the three men rode down into the wash where a calf had been lucky to get out alive, luckier than a man who had not been so fortunate, Charlie quietly noted exactly how the upper reaches of the waterway sluiced down from above in a channel worn round and smooth as a bobsled run. Though the streambed now ran only a trickle, he knew that could change very quickly should there be any rain up-country. In fact, the watercourse did show signs of recent flash flooding, possibly from the previous week's rain in the area. The rush of water had been deep and swift, judging from the debris plastered along the walls of the watercourse.

As the three rode farther up the narrowing canyon, it became apparent what had lured the unfortunate young archaeologist to the area. The canyon walls held scattered pictographs and even some engraved petroglyphs at nearly every turn, some of them from quite early times, and not of the usual type found this far south.

Following the steep course of the streambed, the three Navajo came at last to the place where R. J. Tyler had set his camp. The dark green splash of cottonwoods was in vivid contrast to the vermillion of the canyon walls, and a light trickle of water turned to mist as it tumbled over the edge at the upper end of the little gorge. There was the fire-ring and a few tent stakes still in the ground along with a bit of stacked firewood. The camp had been set back from the water, which gathered in a pool and then plunged to the next lower level. The spot seemed well chosen, far enough below the canyon rim to be invisible to the casual observer, but above the most violent runoff. R. J. had known something about setting a camp in that country. The site was now covered by the tracks of the recovery team, and as Charlie had surmised, little had been left undisturbed.

Harley gave no more than a cursory glance at the campsite and immediately moved upstream to a series of deep slick-rock basins, known locally as "potholes." Though the stream was now no more than a trickle, the larger depressions still held a good bit of water. When Thomas caught up, Harley was on his knees, his nose nearly touching the smooth sandstone edge of the largest bowl, and Thomas watched through narrowed eyes to see for himself what the tracker might find.

Charlie wandered beyond the camp and seemed more interested in the primordial images scrawled on the rock walls than more recent happenings. Since his early days at UNM he had sustained a serious interest in the ancient history of the area, had in fact been tempted to switch his major from law to archaeology. Even now he maintained a correspondence with his former archaeology professor, Dr. George Custer, a man he had come to admire.

Charlie tried to imagine the primal wall art through the eyes of R. J. Tyler and wondered what that unfortunate might have made of them in his last hours. Not all authorities held the same opinion regarding the meaning of even the more common of the designs.

Harley Ponyboy, calling his name from upstream, startled him. The echo from the canyon walls made the summons sound even more urgent.

"Charlie, there's something you need to see up here!"

Thomas was already at Harley's side and gazed along with him into the largest of the catch basins, which sat below quite a steep overhang in the watercourse. During times of even distant rain, water might come gushing down this sluiceway and over the edge in a virtual torrent. Harley had spotted a little niche in the rock wall surround, almost hidden by a sprig of sage growing from a crack. Harley reached into the fissure and produced a well used bar of soap.

"Soap," Harley declared, stating the obvious, but proud of the discovery nonetheless. "If the sun had not been exactly right, I would'n never have seen it. That guy was taking a shower in this pothole before the flash flood hit. Probably never heard it coming until it was too late." He beamed, "That's why he was naked! Why, he was probably just washed downstream 'til he got sucked into the quicksand. That's what probably happened to him."

Charlie knelt and examined the bar of soap and looked up at the little waterfall still tinkling over the edge, and nodded, "Just could be, I guess."

Thomas rose and stepped back with a frown. "This still doesn't explain what happened to the guy's stuff."

Charlie agreed with Thomas to some extent too. "No, but at least now we're just talking petty theft rather than murder."

"Maybe." Thomas seemed unconvinced. "But I still think we should make a circle and see what kind of sign we can cut upstream." He hesitated and thought back. "Coming in here the first time, Harley and I didn't cross any man or horse tracks, yet it's certain someone else *was* through here, so they must have come cross-country, above us, at some point." He thought for a moment and then hedged, "This canyon floor is nearly all slick-rock. I suppose a person who knew what he was doing could pass through without leaving much sign, especially with these recent rains that washed everything away." It was true, even tracks of game and livestock had been nearly obliterated.

They had to travel nearly two miles above the camp site before Harley found even a recognizable footprint, and that, in the soft sand of a feeder wash; a print made by a very worn but common work shoe, by the look of it. Only the one print was discernable, and it was angling down toward R. J. Tyler's campsite. They searched for almost another mile before the next tracks turned up, these made by a hiking boot that headed back north up the streambed toward Teec Nos Pos. These tracks were not hard to follow, as though the person knew the different boot prints had changed his signature. Harley noted that both of the two different prints they'd found were of nearly the same size, the first possibly only a half-size smaller than the second. Even the new prints gradually petered out due to the heavier rain that occurred higher up. They had totally disappeared by the time the men reached the head of the canyon and a trailhead... but this was not the trailhead where they had left the truck and horse trailer.

If Harley remembered Charlie's topo map correctly, they were still a good way from the truck. "Hold up, guys!" he called to the other two as he stepped off Shorty. Thomas's horse had apparently thought they were headed for home and, as horses will, had picked up the pace. Charlie's horse had stayed right with the piebald, and both were now well out in front of Harley, whose mule knew quite well this was not their trailhead, and that there were likely hours of tough canyon going ahead of them.

Shorty, in no particular hurry now, closed his eyes and rested his weight on three legs. Lop-eared, he awaited some sort of a decision. Harley dug through his saddlebag and produced the well-creased topo map from that morning. It didn't take him long to figure out there was still an additional drainage between them and their truck. He motioned the others to come back and said simply, "We're far enough tis way."

Thomas shook his head. "I figured we might still hit that track again a little farther on."

"Not likely," Harley replied scanning a terrain that continued to gain elevation. "First off, the rain was heaviest up here and didn't leave much sign. Second, this trail is just going ta take us higher up the mountain." He paused and again looked upcountry. "Something tells me this guy we're following doesn't know this country any better than we do... It's almost like he's jus' wandering around, but keeps heading generally north. I thought first he might have a vehicle at this trailhead... If he did, he's gone... or maybe he's jus' looking for a ride out of here."

Thomas pushed his hat back and adjusted his weight in the stirrups. "...Or maybe he thought he would find R. J. Tyler's vehicle up here. I'm sure he could have backtracked him out of that canyon before the rains got too heavy; he seems pretty savvy to me."

Charlie weighed in, "Since we know R. J.'s wife was going to pick him up and he had no vehicle, this person, if he was the one involved at all, didn't find any car keys in that camp down there, so he probably wasn't looking for a vehicle. Looks more like he was trying to lose himself out here." Doubt had begun to worry the back edge of Charlie's mind, and he was becoming less certain of his "accidental death" theory.

"No, but very few people out here take their keys with them... too easy to lose. Not a good thing in the middle of nowhere." Thomas wasn't ready to concede the point and enjoyed arguing with Charlie in any case. "Most hide them in one of those little black key box thingies... or maybe just put 'em up under the bumper." He smiled. "...You know, like you do."

Charlie smiled, too, and had to agree. His own keys were hidden under the front bumper in a black plastic magnetic box in case someone got separated or should return before the others.

Harley grinned. "I always thought it was funny how people did that... and with everyone else knowing they do it too. Doesn't make much sense, does it?" He chuckled as he put the map away. "I always just left my keys in the truck... back when I had a truck... back when I had a license to drive one." The smile left his face as he pondered this progression of events from his drinking days.

Thomas looked over at him. "I remember that truck. It was the one with the bumper sticker that said I SURVIVED BOARDING SCHOOL. He chuckled. "I doubt it was ever in any danger of being stolen... As I recall, you eventually had to pay the wrecking yard to come get it."

Harley frowned across his saddle at Thomas and changed the subject. "We only got about an hour more light; that's gonna put us back at the vehicle a good ways after dark." Harley didn't like crossing strange country at night. Too easy to get rimmed up and end up spending a night out.

Not that he hadn't done it before, but that didn't mean he wanted to do it again. And, too, there was still that possibility of a *chindi* roaming around out there, somewhere… just waiting to jump on a person.

Harley led the way and assured them he had the route pretty much set in his mind. He thought they could work their way around the upper end of the watershed that still separated them from their vehicle. Thomas and Charlie fell in behind the mule, which for the first time felt it was on the right track for home, and picked up the pace accordingly. The two horses weren't convinced and wanted to stay on the main trail. They were hungry, too, but like most good trail horses knew better than try to eat along the way. It was nearly sundown when the trio hit the big sage flats that divided the watersheds. Harley pointed out a scattered band of sheep, watched for a moment, and knew almost instantly something was wrong. They were all over the place, obviously without a herder, and no dog in sight. You didn't often see that in this country. The three of them scanned the horizon, but it was Thomas who first saw the old woman. He had to look twice, thinking he might have imagined the movement at the upper end of the flats.

When the figure was pointed out to him, Harley reluctantly pulled Shorty to a halt. "Looks like that old lady could use some help with her sheep. Coyotes, or maybe a bear, musta' got into 'em."

Thomas grinned. "Or maybe she just fell asleep and let them get away from her." Then he frowned. "Seems like their dog would have kept them together, though." It was inconceivable to Thomas that someone would have a band of sheep out in this country without a dog. You might get away with that some places, but you wouldn't up here.

The three sat their mounts in silence and peered through the gloom to see what the woman would do about the sheep. To their surprise she came straight through the scattered flock and was obviously headed their way. She seemed to pay no heed to the sheep whatsoever and was making good time across the broken sage flats.

Charlie sighed and said, "I guess we better go see what she wants. Looks to me like she might have a problem." The three rode abreast toward the old woman, who seeing them finally heading her way, broke into a shuffling run. As she drew near, the men could see she was quite clearly exhausted and somewhat unsteady on her feet.

"*Yaa 'eh t'eeh*," Harley called, though she was still some way off.

"I don't think she can hear you yet, Harley." Thomas cocked his head at the old woman. "There's something bad happened, I think," and kicked his horse into a lope, with the others close behind. The woman stopped short and waited for Thomas to come to a sliding stop. He was off the horse before it could even regain its feet, and stood in front of the old woman amazed. She looked even older than he first guessed. Her head was lifted and she sucked in great gulps of air, unable to speak—barely able to stay on her feet. He took her arm to steady her and spoke quietly in Navajo as the others moved closer. "Easy, *shimásáni*, rest a little and catch your breath. You should not be running so hard at your age."

There were tears of relief in the old woman's eyes as she realized these men intended to help her. She went almost to her knees, but Harley caught her other arm, and between them he and Thomas supported her and patted her on the back to help with her breathing.

When the old woman had calmed somewhat and re-gained the ability to speak, she peered from one to the other and asked them in Navajo, "Have you seen my granddaugh-ter hereabouts, *shiy'ké*?" using the old Navajo word for *my sons*. "I cannot find her, though I have searched since before daylight. She did not come back last night with the sheep, and the dog came in early this morning and was badly cut in two places. That dog, he died right away after he came in, and I do not know now where he left my granddaughter. He never lets her out of his sight and would not ordinarily come back without her."

She raised her hands to her face, and the men were afraid she would cry again, but she didn't, only wiped her eyes on her sleeve. "This is all too much for an old woman. We are alone, the two of us out here, now that my husband is gone. This girl is all I have. I don't have no one else, only my granddaughter." Charlie and Thomas looked at one another and something passed between them that the old woman caught a sense of. She peered hopefully at the two. "Do you know something about this, my boys? Have you seen the girl?" She shaded her eyes with one hand, gazed out across the country, then went on in a low voice almost as though talking to herself, "Her mother sent her to stay with me until I arrange my life and sell the stocks and all. We wanted to wait until end of summer, when the lamb price might go up." All the time the old woman was talking she watched in every direction, searching the horizon.

"Where is your *hogan,* Grandmother...? Are you close by?" Charlie's Navajo was not as good as the others, but he understood the woman and felt his heart sink as he thought what might have happened to her granddaughter.

Thomas and Harley remained silent and waited for her answer.

The old woman straightened slightly. She did not return Charlie's gaze, but did appear to settle herself, and finally replied, "I am She Has Horses." She used her Navajo name, as she could see all three men understood the language *not everyone did these days*. She raised an arm and it went crimson in the brilliant glow of the setting sun. "We are over there, only a short way, on the edge of Little Salt, above Water Comes Running." The woman had now said all she could manage for the moment and grew quiet.

Charlie shook his head saying, "I'm going to have to go back to the truck and call this in." He looked up at the darkening sky and then to his friends. "Maybe you two could help this woman gather her sheep and get them home. Harley, you might let her ride Shorty—I doubt she can ride Thomas's horse, and it doesn't look like she's up to walking much farther. Maybe she'll have something for you to eat." He concentrated on the task before him. "I'm close enough now that I can find the truck. I'll take the topo map—I've got a flashlight in my saddlebags. I'll be back up here with the truck and trailer as soon as I can, but it might be morning before it's light enough to find this place again." He threw Thomas a warning glance as Harley retrieved the map. "You be careful tonight. I'm having some second thoughts about all this." With that, he clapped Harley lightly on the shoulder, took the map, and swung into the saddle. He nudged the sorrel to a ground-eating trot, a gait that seemed to suit the horse. He suspected he could have Search and Rescue out there by morning, possibly, even before he himself would make it back.

5

*The Wreck*

When the van flung itself off the road and rolled over and over to the bottom of the arroyo, the six illegals sleeping in back were battered and thrown from top to bottom—two of them partially out windows—and one thrown through the big sliding door when the latch failed. The *mojado* had not ridden in many cars but figured if the driver was buckled in there had to be a good reason for it. Luca had been fortunate to be in the seat beside the driver and also buckled in. It was not luck, exactly. He had demanded the seat and no one was man enough to argue. He got sick riding in the back, he told them, though he didn't have to tell them anything at all. They'd seen the homemade prison tattoos on his neck and forearms, knew the significance of the designs, and guessed how he came to be there. They had also seen the thin switchblade knife he used to cut the apple the driver had given him at the rest stop. The *coyotero* was a cautious man and wanted to stay on the good side of this obviously dangerous passenger. He would have much preferred the company of one of the two young women in the group, but both had earlier turned down that opportunity.

There were no other seatbelts, so only Luca and the *coyotero* were spared the worst of the deadly crash. It would not have been quite so bad if the juniper tree had not been in their flight path, but it was, and it nearly broke the airborne vehicle in half.

When he recovered from the initial shock and gut-wrenching jolt of the seat belt, he found his right arm had at some point been caught between the twisted door and the frame and now had no feeling. He didn't think the arm was broken—perhaps it would get better in time. It was good, he supposed, that he was left-handed. It was now clear none of the other six illegals would make it, though one young woman was taking shallow, rattling breaths, and mouthing what he took to be a prayer. Prayers would not help her this night.

Truly, he thought, God worked in mysterious ways. He had been worried that some of these people might eventually talk about the tattooed man whose face had been all over Mexican television. The news of the escape had dominated the media in Sonora State.

He looked over at the driver, who was breathing heavily, unconscious, or more likely in shock. He was bleeding profusely from head wounds inflicted by the shattered window glass. In the green glow of the instruments, particles embedded in the man's scalp glimmered like emeralds. Maybe the *coyotero* would live, provided someone reported the accident in a timely manner. This highway 491 between Gallup and Shiprock was a lonely stretch, especially at night, but that was why the *coyotero* had chosen the back-way into Colorado in the first place. No one wanted to be on this road late at night. There were no "profilers" out here—tribal police had not had the benefit of that training, and rightly so, most thought.

He felt under the seat for the tire iron he'd seen earlier when they had stopped at the abandoned rest area. It didn't take much, a hard rap behind the ear of the stirring driver and worry of discovery in this new country was greatly reduced.

He didn't know exactly where he was but had looked over the driver's shoulder as he studied the roadmap outside Douglas. It was a circuitous route, highlighted in yellow, one carefully thought out. The *coyotero* had good luck with it in the past and had no reason to think it would be otherwise this time.

Luca did remember the driver saying this was one of the largest Indian reservations in world, but that didn't bother him. He was mestizo himself, not so different from these people, who themselves had a long history with the Mexicans. He had no way of knowing it, but there was even a clan, *Naakaii dine'é*, The Mexican People, still heavy in that blood some imagined. In the old times there was much trading and stealing of women on both sides. Some even figured this ongoing "*molina de sangre*," with the Mexicans and others was responsible for the continued strength of the *Diné*—one of the few North American tribes on the increase.

When at last he was able to extricate himself from the gore of the mangled van, he was surprised that, aside from the arm, everything seemed in order. His legs were bruised and his knees hurt from being shoved up under the dash, but for the most part he was better off than he had any right to be, but then, he had always been lucky that way, and no one could say why.

He did know he should probably get away from the accident as quickly as possible, and after a quick look around for the roadmap, which he could not find, he grabbed one of the milk jugs of water from the wreckage and headed for the nearby but rugged country of the Carrizo mountains to the west. Ultimately he must turn more northward, but for now it was best to lose himself in that isolated area he remembered from the map. It was mid-summer, he'd grown up in this kind of country, he would be fine here—but no one must know. That was the key.

~~~~~~~

When Charlie finally returned to the old woman's *hogan* the next morning, there were several trucks in the yard. The girl's body had already been found. The dogs had taken only an hour and forty-five minutes to locate her, stuffed in a cleft of a rock outcropping. The opening had been walled up to hide the body, but it was a rough job and the hounds had no trouble going directly to it. A volunteer rode a four-wheeler back to tell the old woman the news, and though he was trained in such things, it had been difficult for both of them. He had been told Charlie would likely already be there, and filled him in on the morning's happenings. He was the group's EMT, he said, but when he had seen he wouldn't be needed, offered to go back and inform the anxious old woman that her granddaughter wouldn't be coming back. After she had gone back inside the *hogan* to fix the men coffee (no situation was so cruel a guest couldn't be offered something to eat or drink). Charlie asked the EMT what they had found.

The man didn't answer at first, only shook his head and stared back the way he had come. He was surprisingly young, and Charlie imagined the thing was hard for him, and so didn't push him, instead just asked if he had seen Thomas and Harley.

"Yes, they showed us to where the sheep were when they first came across them last evening. It only took the dogs about an hour to find her from there." He exhaled loudly and then took his time explaining exactly how things were out there. The girl had been slashed repeatedly with a large knife, a butcher knife maybe. The medic had been in residence at the clinic in Shiprock for over a year and had seen his share of knife wounds, but none like this. "It seemed almost like she was killed in some sort of mindless fury. She had been stabbed several times, even after she was dead, already bled out... The stab wounds were clean... didn't bleed," he said.

The medic was interrupted by two other grim-faced volunteers returning on four-wheelers, with the search dogs footsore and tired out, trailing behind. They loaded the hounds and were gone without speaking to anyone. The old woman, She Has Horses, stood forlornly at the *hogan* door, gesturing with the coffeepot and watching them go. Her features took on a vacant expression as she returned, unseeing, to the quiet refuge of the dwelling.

Her dog, the one that came home to die, was still where the old woman laid him in the brush shelter next to the *hogan*—her "summer *hogan*" she called it. Charlie and the medic went for a look, and according to the EMT the wounds appeared pretty much the same as those suffered by the girl.

The medic followed Charlie back to the *hogan*, where they thanked the old lady for the coffee and moved out of earshot.

The medic seemed hesitant. "We're only here in a search and rescue capacity...or recovery in this case. Your investigators, the tall one anyway, said they would try to find where she was killed and what happened. The chunky little guy wrote everything down in a notebook, and then they just rode off. They seemed to know what they were doing. A couple of our people will stay with the remains until law enforcement arrives." He shrugged. "Your guys are still out there doing whatever it is they do, I guess."

Charlie didn't change expression or give any indication he was surprised by this information, just nodded, and after gulping his coffee, waved goodbye to She Has Horses, then went directly to the trailer and re-saddled the gelding. *Those two will be my undoing. I'm sure of it now.*

Harley Ponyboy and Thomas Begay had the only horses out there, so they weren't hard to follow, even for someone like Charlie. When he caught up with them, they were already halfway back to the old woman's place.

Harley, who was out in front, saw the look on Charlie's face and immediately avowed, "It was not my fault!" He gave Thomas a hard look. "He just took over like he always does. What else could I do?" Charlie didn't even look at him as he rode past.

Thomas Begay sat his horse, waiting for the inevitable. "Now, Charlie... buddy... before you say anything..."

"YOU, don't say another word." Charlie's voice had an edge. "How in the hell did you think you could pull this off? You two don't even look like investigators."

Thomas shrugged and looked down at his saddle horn. "Yeah, that's what *they* said too," then brightened, "But they ain't the law either... They didn't really care." He winked. "We probably won't hear any more about it."

Charlie shook his head. "You better hope you don't. Do you know what kind of trouble you two could get into impersonating a law officer?"

"We never impersonated no one." He waggled a finger at Charlie. "I told them *you* were an investigator with Legal Services, and we worked for *you*. That's all I said—they were the ones who thought... whatever it was they thought."

Charlie sighed, rubbed his forehead with the back of his hand and shook his head.

"Look at the upside, Charlie. This time we were first at the crime scene. We didn't mess it up neither. And we discovered a few things that no one else might have caught..."

Charlie snorted. "First of all, you and Harley were first at the *last* 'crime scene,' ...and if you hadn't been afraid of dead people, we might have learned something that would have prevented *this* murder. And secondly, anything you may have found out here is considered evidence. You could be charged with tampering. You two are digging yourself a hole—one I may not be able to pull you out of." Charlie whirled the sorrel and rode off at a lope.

Harley quietly looked over at Thomas. "I tol' you it was a bad idea."

Thomas watched Charlie ride off. "Maybe... maybe not."

Charlie had covered no more than a hundred yards when Thomas saw his horse slow, come to a stop, and finally turn around. He looked over at Harley and raised an eyebrow.

When the three tied their horses and went on foot to where the girl was killed, Harley gave his version of what the sign revealed. He moved slowly, carefully, and addressed each point in a low voice, as though reassessing the information for his own benefit. "This person came up on the far edge of the band, from behind that oak brush," he said and pointed to a few scraggly young scrub oaks. "The sheep were spread out, and this lamb maybe strayed apart from the others. This was someone who knew how to move around stock, and he clubbed it before it knew what hit it. He didn't bother to gut it, and by the time the dog discovered him, he was cutting up meat." Harley carefully considered the next part. In his mind's eye he could almost see it happen and nodded to himself before going on. "The dog probably started barking and raising hell to attract the girl, who could not have been far behind. By its tracks it was not a big dog and did not confront the man close up—until the girl showed up and most likely urged it on. That gave the dog courage, and it was then it must have rushed him." Harley knew a lot about dogs, and sheep, and herders. "I expect this fellow knew how to handle a knife. I doubt the dog did much damage before going down. The girl didn't stop to think, just jumped in to help the dog. She probably had a stick or a quirt but had no idea what she was dealing with... and that was the end of her." Harley rubbed his chin and looked into the distance... "The bastard knew she was done and watched her crawl away. Just finished his meat cutting, with the same knife, like nothing happened. The girl headed for those rocks over there—maybe trying to get away and hide. She didn't make it." And this was the part that bothered Harley Ponyboy most: "Only after he finished cutting what he wanted off the lamb did he go over and stab the girl a couple more times. The medic thought she was pretty much dead by the time she was stabbed." Harley hesitated. "She was a strong girl and had a lot of heart, I guess. She crawled quite a ways."

Thomas nodded and finished the scenario for him; "He dragged her on over to that outcropping and walled her up in that big crack over there. The dog must have got away cause we didn't see any sign of him—went off and died somewhere is my guess. We found little patches of black and white hair cut off short, but no dog." Thomas looked Charlie straight in the eye (something the Navajo try to avoid) and pointed to tracks in the sand near the rock outcropping. "Those are the same hiking boot prints we found above R. J. Tyler's campsite. This is a bad man by anyone's standards. And I don't think we've heard the last of him neither."

Harley moved closer and touched Charlie Yazzie on the shoulder. "If someone don' get this guy soon… this is gonna happen again."

No one spoke on the way back to She Has Horses' camp. As they came in sight of the *hogan*, two tribal police vehicles were pulling out. The lead SUV stopped and rolled down the window.

Samuel Shorthair leaned out and flagged Charlie over. "We'd a been here sooner, but we ran into a few problems." He cut his eyes at the man in the suit next to him. "Agent Mayfield here said we needed to wait on the forensic guys out of Farmington. They're in the other truck with Billy Red Clay. The S&R boys radioed we would have to go around the head of the canyon and said it would be rough going. I expect we'll be out here most of the day." He smiled at Charlie and indicated the horses. "Looks like you boys came prepared." He looked past Charlie, recognized Thomas, and lifted a finger at him. *"Yaa' eh t'eeh*, Begay… long time since government school."

Thomas nodded but didn't smile.

Harley lagged back, pretended to be busy with his saddle strings, and didn't look up. He didn't like police in general and had heard questionable stories about Samuel Shorthair from Thomas.

Samuel Shorthair studied Harley a moment, then turned his attention back to Charlie. "Dispatch said you told them you would stay till we got up here, and we appreciate that." He was already rolling up the window as he spoke… and then remembered something else and rolled it back down. "I don't know if you've heard, but there was a van went off the road a couple of days ago down on 491 between Newcomb and the Sanostee turn off. Illegals, apparently, rollover, no survivors as far as we know, but we may have to rethink that in view of recent happenings. The time frame was right and so was the general area... just something to keep in mind."

FBI Agent Eldon Mayfield looked across Sam and directly at Charlie. "We'd appreciate it if you boys didn't mix in on this one. There's a full contingent of federal people on the way up here along with more tribal police and a tracker with fresh dogs. They are due at Teec Nos Pos any minute, according to the radio, and headed this way. Another bunch from Kayenta are coming in from the Dinnehotso side and yet others from Chinle will come in from Tesaile to the south. We think we've got things pretty well covered."

Sam Shorthair gave Charlie a secret wink. "Yep, the FBI ought to have him boxed in shortly. Me and Billy Red Clay were going to borrow the S&R boy's four-wheelers and get after him from here, but now they're saying they don't think we'll get very far if he heads back into the Carizzos." He put the truck in gear and started to pull out.

Charlie motioned for him to wait. "One other thing, Sam. The girl's grandmother is worried she will have to identify the body. Apparently, one of the rescue team told her it might be required... You know how that is... These old people are afraid. The girl's cousin from Mexican Water should be here to help the old lady before long. He'd probably be better for that job."

Sam thought about it and looked over at Agent Mayfield, who first shook his head, but then sighed and grunted okay. As he pulled away, the tribal policeman looked again at Harley Ponyboy and nodded as though he finally recognized him and might say something... but then didn't. He just gunned the engine and was gone.

Harley urged his mule up between the two horses. "So, does this mean he expects us ta go home now?"

Thomas watched the two trucks jounce their way up the rocky track and smiled. "What he expects, and what he gets, might be two different things."

# 6

*The FBI*

The vehicle was barely out of sight of the three mounted Navajos when FBI Agent Eldon Mayfield turned to Sam Shorthair. "So, that's Charlie Yazzie?" He gazed out the window with the look of one displeased but without grounds for being so. *So that's the person responsible for me being posted to this god-forsaken jurisdiction.*

"That's him alright. I guess you could say he's the one that brought down your predecessor." Sam said this as though he knew what the agent was thinking, and paused to gauge his reaction.

"I've read the files. Agent Davis made his own bed. There are always a few rotten apples... He was worse than most, I guess." Agent Mayfield had suffered a considerable lack of cooperation in his new job due mostly to the previous agent's indiscretions... murder being only one of them.

"Charlie's been in on several other high-profile cases since then and has become a pretty big man at Legal Services." Sam said this with only a hint of envy. "Pretty much writes his own ticket, from what I hear." A thoughtful expression was on the policeman's face when he added, "The funny thing is, he never actually seems to solve a case... but he's always there when it solves itself—kind of like Clark Kent after Superman leaves."

The FBI man frowned. "That's what I hear, too." And this time it was plain he wasn't pleased.

"Oh, he has a law degree and all," Sam went on, "but there's more to it than that. Charlie truly has the wellbeing of the Navajo people at heart, really cares about what happens to them. He could have gone anywhere and done well, but apparently thought he could do the most good here on the reservation." He smiled. "There's not enough of us that think that way anymore." Sam paused. "There's even talk of him running for council, though I'm not sure he's geared that way. I know one thing. It would throw a monkey wrench in the 'good old boy pass-along-system' out here. Charlie don't knuckle under like some; I suspect he would face some strong opposition from the old guard."

"So you know him pretty well then?"

"I guess so, as well as anyone out here can know another, I suppose." Sam turned to the agent. "He and I, and Thomas, all went to boarding school together. I was a couple of years ahead of them." He turned his attention back to the road in time to avoid a water-cut deep enough to wreck the truck's front end, and was lucky to stop in time. "Charlie's all right... I've always liked him." He put the vehicle in four-wheel drive, dropped into low gear, and eased across the hazard all in one smooth motion. "Thomas is something else again. Heavy drinker for several years, ran with the wrong people, and generally made a mess of a life that could have turned out a lot differently. He's smart and people like him." He shifted the suv up a gear. "Looks like he's turned himself around now... We'll see."

"What about the little fat guy?"

"Harley?" Sam chuckled glancing side-eyed at the agent's girth. "Harley's something. He went to a different boarding school than we did... that is, when they could catch him and make him go at all. He's from old-time, hardcore traditional Navajo, up in Monument Valley. His people kept him out of school as much as they could—said they needed him to help with the sheep. He's probably the last of that generation who follow the old path. He and Thomas were the original drinking buddies... in and out of jail a lot... He's clean now, for the most part. There's more to him than meets the eye. He and Thomas are a lot alike."

~~~~~~

At the *hogan* of She Has Horses, Harley fed Shorty and the two horses what hay was left in the trailer, and threw down another two bales off the top rack for the old woman's sheep. They hadn't been fed since the previous night and were now noisily milling around the corral, certain they had been forgotten.

At the old lady's insistence, the men again drank coffee and ate hot fry-bread from a tin platter. She hovered around them as though in a daze, asking again and again if she could get them something more to eat. "I'm thanking you for feeding those sheep, grandsons. They were sure getting hungry, I guess." She gestured across at the corrals. "Those lambs were already dragging the ewes down. When ewes don't eat, they use up their fat pretty quick and have nothing left to make milk." The old lady reminded Charlie of his own grandmother—spoke in the same broken way old people talked when he was a boy. She kept talking, wouldn't stop, afraid the men might leave her there alone before the "laws" returned and asked her to identify her dead granddaughter. She couldn't bear to see the child. No matter how close one was to the deceased, or how good a person they had been, there still was the belief the person's *chindi* might do them some harm. Already she avoided saying her granddaughter's name—even though some Navajo make allowance for a four-day mourning period. The old woman, like many traditionalists, thought it best to put the dead out of her mind as quickly as possible.

The three men watched... and knew. In olden times it was thought the dead had a journey to make, one they had to make alone, and the living should no longer dwell on them lest it attract their *chindi* and cause other evils, even cast shadows over everyone's *hozoji*. They thought it best to concentrate on the living. These were beliefs passed down from the old wandering times in the far north when people, living and dead, had to be left behind for the good of the many. Some early anthropologists thought the belief in what some call the "*chindi* phenomena" came about to alleviate the guilt involved in abandoning the dead. Others ventured the guess that it was engendered by the need to avoid the spreading of disease in times of pestilence. There were other theories as well, but these seemed chief among those at academic conferences.

The Navajo tribe is said to be the most studied group of Indians in America, and the running joke among anthropologists was that the typical Navajo family consists of a mother, a father, children, and an anthropologist. Indian families were sometimes talked into allowing professional observers into their homes for cultural studies and were generally paid for the privilege of doing so. After a while of this easy money some families became tied to the stipend and would do almost anything to avoid giving it up… including making up things they thought researchers would like to hear. Several early papers on the subject have been discredited for this very reason.

Thomas was always a little leery of his Uncle John Nez's white anthropologist wife, Marissa, and what she might be writing down of his or Lucy Tallwoman's comments about traditional Navajo life. Many of those things were secret traditions or ceremonies, and not for just any outsider to interpret. Marissa had been fond of catching old Paul T'Sosi when he was alone, and trying to extract certain information she thought pertinent to her studies. She knew he had studied to be a singer but figured he might be induced to impart some knowledge of the ceremonies he had learned as a boy. Since he was never really a singer, she told him it might be all right to let her in on a few traditions, at least in regard to the women's part in those things. She soon found Paul T'Sosi no easy mark, and later turned her attention to Lucy Tallwoman, who seemed more inclined to be cooperative when properly approached. Lucy thought it important that a woman's view should be made known for future generations to figure into the mix. It was not often women were given that chance, she thought.

Harley Ponyboy and Thomas Begay were of the opinion the person responsible for the girl's horrendous death should be pursued immediately, before he could do more harm or get clear out of the country. They discussed the matter with Charlie and were a little surprised when he agreed.

"I thought it over," Charlie admitted, "there in the truck last night, and had dispatch notify Sue. She'll call Lucy Tallwoman and get in touch with Anita. I told her we might not be back for a couple of days." Charlie looked from one to the other of them. "Anyone who wants to go home can take the truck and trailer and just pick me up when this is over." Charlie always carried a blanket and something to eat behind the back seat of the truck, just in case. It was big country and, should the unexpected happen, could be a treacherous one as well.

The old woman, who had again been listening from the doorway, stepped outside. "It is only right, my grandsons, that you should try to catch this person who has come through here killing and hurting our hearts like this. I can help you with blankets and food, you are welcome to them, and I sure will thank you to take what you need." She turned back into the *hogan* and soon they heard a banging of pans and the clunk of cans thrown into a burlap bag.

The old woman later told them she would go to live with her sister now, and the two of them would help each other forget her granddaughter, if they could. She had a school picture of the girl somewhere. She must remember to find it and burn it along with those pitiful few things the girl had left behind. She held a great rage in her heart for the person who had caused this evil, and while she knew it was wrong and might affect her *hozo*, she hoped there would be a reckoning while she still lived to see it.

Charlie kept an eye on the weather as they gathered such gear as they had. There were signs of a front moving in. The high and wispy "mares' tails" sketched across the turquoise of the summer sky told him they had best be moving along; these were one of the most reliable signs of an impending frontal system, ordinarily within twenty-four to forty-eight hours, and generally sooner rather than later.

The other agencies would be out in force within hours, and everyone in the country would soon be alerted. To Charlie's way of thinking, a few hours head start might make all the difference. He had a feeling this person had been on the run before and catching him would not be easy. They had only the one gun, the .38 snub-nose Smith & Wesson he kept handy in the glove box of his pickup, or in his shoulder holster, should he be horseback. Hopefully, the fugitive had no weapon beyond a knife, and if that was the case, they should be ahead with just the revolver.

~~~~~~~~

Luca Tarango, for that was his name, moved easily under the weight of the pack. He had plenty of freeze-dried food, and while he didn't know that's what it was, he quickly learned how to fix it into some semblance of a meal, even though he could barely read or write, and certainly not in English, which he spoke poorly.

What he really craved was fresh meat. There had been precious little of it these long months. Once he was farther down the trail, he intended to have his fill. He had kept only two or three pounds of back-strap stripped from the lamb carcass, and the added burden was hardly noticeable for a man used to the labor of carrying large stones. He remembered entire mornings carrying the heavy rocks to a certain spot, only to be told in the afternoon that they must be returned to where they were previously. He had been in that place a long time and this, though not easy, was infinitely more to his liking. His uncles had spent a lot of time and money arranging his "escape," not so much because they were his uncles, but because they were afraid not to. They had sold nearly everything they owned to furnish the bribes and the cost of the *coyotero*. Luca was not one to be ignored, and when he asked their help, they knew to refuse him would prove a serious mistake when he did get out... and Luca always got out. And when he did, there was a reckoning.

His recently acquired shoes were too large and would have quickly blistered less callused and hardened feet, but for him they were a blessing, and he was satisfied to have them. It was the same with the other clothing, a bit large, slightly faded and worn, but certainly of a higher caliber than he was accustomed to. He had seen from the start this would be an easy land to get along in, and that one of his abilities might do very well here—with a only a little effort. When he was back with Tressa, he would show what could be accomplished with a little foresight and determination—things so little appreciated where he came from. Tressa might not be too pleased to see him at first, but when her new man was out of the picture it would be different. She had been in the U.S. almost a year now, and while he knew her way had been long, and suspected she had been hard used from time to time, it apparently had proven worth it, judging from her one letter... just as his own journey would eventually be worth it.

The white man down in the canyon had been relatively easy to deal with, even with the handicap of a bad arm. The man had obviously just finished bathing and washing his clothes, and had only just started up from the water when Luca stepped in front of him. The man smiled, embarrassed, at the sight of a stranger who appeared out of nowhere. When Luca showed the switchblade and ordered him to put down his clothes, the man hesitated only a moment. Luca's English was not that good, but the man understood him all right and did as he was told—all the while backing down the few steps to the water. Luca kept gesturing with the knife until he was upon him, and then from his higher vantage, kicked him full in the chest, sending him sprawling backward into the water, where caught off balance the man was swept into the next and deepest pothole. This one was not so far across, but with steeper, slicker sides. The white man was forced to claw at the smooth edges to keep from being swept over the next sheer drop. He struggled desperately to cling to the smooth rock walls, and his fingers bled from the attempt. Finally, he managed one last desperate effort and was able to secure a hold by which he pulled himself partially onto the ledge. Luca dealt him a vicious blow to the head, sending him tumbling over the precipice to the rocky pool below. Then there was only a blob of white, floating face down toward yet another drop off, and that quickly disappeared from sight.

The white man had not shown the courage of the *Indio* girl, or even her dog, once the animal perceived itself to be in the right. Both had acted impulsively, out of instinct, and without thinking. That made it easier for Luca. If the girl had fled, he would have had to run her down, but it would have ended the same. He couldn't afford anyone knowing he was here… not now. Going forward, he could see it would be these *Indios* who would pose the greatest threat.

# 7

## *The Hunt*

"The wind people are out playing ball today!" Harley shouted, pulling up his collar and turning his mule's rear-end to yet another sand-laden gust. Just after noon a cold front had blown in from the north and showed no sign of letting up. It was now nearly too dark to see the trail, and the three *Diné* looked at one another, each hoping the other would suggest finding a place to stop, preferably one out of the wind. While none of the three wanted to be the one to give in, it was Charlie who finally conceded it was getting too dark to go on. The other two quickly concurred and cast about for some shelter from the abrasive blast of the norther.

"There's a little bunch of cedars just up ahead and what looks like an arroyo." Harley peered through the dust and turned Shorty back into the teeth of the gale, urging him past the others. After only a short distance he called back over his shoulder, "It's better than nothing." The three edged off the trail and into the gully, which did afford some shelter, but not much. They tied their horses in the trees and dragged their saddles and blankets under the cutback, which did at least deflect the brunt of the wind. They knew they were in for a miserable night but pawed through the bag of canned goods the old woman had given them, and each plucked out a can, not really caring what it was.

"Good! I got beans." Harley grinned in the failing light. "I like beans, all right."

"Crap, this is some kind of little spaghettis." Thomas poked around in it with his pocketknife. "All mushy too." One would have thought he didn't like it, had they not seen the way he wolfed it down.

Charlie dug out his flashlight and inspected his can. "Creamed Corn?" That was all right by him, and he settled back against his saddle and opened it up with the little pull-tab on top. The old woman had been meticulous in her shopping and nearly every can had a pull-tab—a handy thing for something you might have to eat in the saddle, as a herdsman often did.

"How far you think this guy is ahead of us now?" Thomas asked around a mouthful, as much to himself as anyone else.

Harley set his empty can to the side and thought about it. "Maybe a day. It would be longer if we weren't horseback." He raised his voice above the wind, now fairly ripping through the treetops. "This guy can move, and he don't take no breaks neither."

"We'll get him... or someone else will." Thomas rolled himself in his blanket and turned away. "He's under the gun now... There'll be lots of people looking for him tomorrow." And then, just before drifting off, he whispered, "I hope it's us that gets to him first."

When he woke to the cold grey light of dawn, Charlie Yazzie rolled over in his blankets and stared for a moment at just a sliver of moon hanging above the horizon like a golden scythe. The wind had finally died, leaving a layer of grit and dust on his blankets. He wondered what his son was doing back home in Waterflow. Sue was an early riser, as was the boy. She would be up making coffee for herself and a little kettle of oatmeal for the two of them and, were he there, the three of them would enjoy a quiet hour before he left for work. He was beginning to regret getting mixed up in this case; it was not his job. His job was in the offices of Legal Services, where it was warm and clean, and everything was done on the telephone or by moving pieces of paper around from desk to desk. That was what he trained for. Harley and Thomas were more suited to this than he, who fresh out of high school, had chosen to apply to the university and pursue a career in law—what he thought would be a better way of life. Being a lawyer had sounded good in the beginning; he could be someone, make his grandmother proud of him (though she always said she would have been anyway). He had to admit, though, being outside seemed to strike a chord in him at times and was becoming more to his liking as time went on. The fascination of the chase was in his genes, he supposed—as it had been in a thousand generations of his forebears.

Harley Ponyboy was up early gathering dead cedar twigs for a small fire. A strong breeze was again building from the north, and the odor of smoke would flow downwind and alert no one to their presence. He thought briefly of his clan mother, She Has Horses, down below in the sage flats and hoped her sister and nephew had come for her. Her sheep would have to be driven a long way this day before the buyer from Becklabito could pick them up in his stock truck. He wondered at this old woman, only recently met, yet how she was like his own mother through the magic of kinship and clan. This was the lure of the reservation and his people—they were all of the same cloth and their fates intertwined. No matter how far away one might travel or how different the life, still, they remained a part of the whole. Harley was not one to consciously think about these things, but when he did, he liked for them to make sense, and this did. He was where he was supposed to be; he was on the *beauty path*. He looked over at Charlie and wondered if *he* would ever return to the *beauty way* and follow the *path* as he had as a child.

Thomas Begay didn't sleep well and had dreams of evil spirits who changed shapes and disappeared at will. In wakeful interludes he desperately hoped this wasn't some witch or

*Yeenaaldiooshii* they were chasing. By the time he finally stuck his nose out of the blankets, he could smell coffee brewing in an open pan, and it brought him fully awake and anxious to be away. He thought, *we will have to push hard today; that evil spirit couldn't be far away, at least as the crow flies. Ferreting him out might be another matter however. We will have to have our wits about us.*

Lucy Tallwoman had not wanted him to go on this "wild goose chase," as she put it. "What do you think you can do out there that the authorities can't?" she said this tapping her foot on the hard, packed floor of the *hogan*.

Thomas had no answer for that and could only say, "We'll just have to wait and see, won't we?" It was a foolish thing to offer, and he immediately regretted saying it, but it was all he had.

Lucy's father, Old Man Paul T'Sosi, as he was now called, had sat there on the edge of his cot with a frown but had watched with more than a little interest. Lucy was a stubborn woman and Thomas knew he would have to watch his step if he didn't want his saddle set outside the door. It was not even his saddle. He had only borrowed the saddle from Paul and knew the old man probably frowned because his daughter's husband didn't even own a saddle. *He was probably thinking maybe he should just give me the saddle then he could at least go in the knowledge his son-in-law owned his own saddle… and that his daughter could divorce him by setting it outside the hogan.*

Thus the three *Dinè*, each with his own thoughts, huddled around the fire and waited for first light. The man they followed probably had no idea R. J. Tyler's body had been found, but he had to know the shepherd girl would be quickly missed. Once the alarm was raised, the killer might well think he had nothing left to lose and strike again in his determination to escape. No one knew what he looked like, or where he came from, or even how he came to be in that country.

66

The weather was mild, and the man might choose to head further up into the sparsely populated Carrizo highlands, lie low for a while, and wait out that first intensive wave of searchers, something he knew was sure to come.

In any case, Charlie thought the three of *them* were in the best position to intercept him or at least keep track of him until authorities could be informed. He knew there were a few isolated summer camps scattered here and there—in all but the most remote areas. There was good grazing up there most summers, and herders, like the old woman down below, would be following the grass until the snow drove them down.

Harley sipped his coffee from his supper can and thought he still could taste last night's beans. In the breaking dawn he looked across the hazy lower reaches of the Carrizos, and farther out toward the great flying ship of the desert, barely discernable now, as though adrift on a once barren and ancient sea. Early white settlers named it Ship Rock, but few then thought it really looked like a ship. Old Navajo still said *Tse Bit'a'I, "The Rock With Wings,"* and believed their people had been delivered into this country on the back of that great bird—before Monster Slayer turned it to stone. There were many such myths from ancient times, just as there are in the distant past of any people. Harley Ponyboy had great faith in these legends passed down from his ancestors but had a harder time believing some of the stories told by local missionaries.

Harley and Thomas were some of the few younger people who still held to the old ways. That was why old people liked them. When the old woman back at the *hogan* learned he was a Reed People, she took Harley aside and told him she was also *Lòk'aa' Dine'é*, or Reed People, just as he was, and called him her grandson and told him that should he run across others of the clan, he should mention her name and say he was there to help her. "Come right out and tell them you are my grandson. There are lots of Reed People hereabouts. Those are your people, too, and will surely give you anything you have need of, and they will tell you exactly what they know." She cast a furtive glance at Charlie Yazzie. "Do not send in that one with the badge. They might not trust him and may even tell him something that is wrong."

Harley told her he would be sure to do those things, should he get a chance, thanked her, and spoke to her thereafter as he would his own grandmother. To his people's way of thinking, a clan member was close family, and was addressed just so. A person might have many mothers or fathers among the elders of their clan and treat them as such. That was the way it had always been.

Thomas pawed through the grub sack again and found a neatly wrapped package of fresh cornbread the old woman had included. He broke off pieces, which he passed to the other two. "I expect this might be all we have time for this morning, so we better eat it slow and enjoy it."

Harley was still somewhat miffed at Thomas, looked him straight in the eye and crammed his entire portion into his mouth at once, then turned to study the trail. "That wind covered up a lot of sign last night," he mumbled through the mouthful of dry cornbread. Thomas and Charlie just looked at one another, as neither could understand a word he was saying.

Charlie shook out his blankets and watched in the direction the search parties would come. Most likely they would be at the trailheads already, some on four-wheelers, a few horseback, but most on foot. They would work in pairs or small groups and be well armed, and they would be cautioned to use their radios to keep in touch. No one would be allowed to go off on his own—not with this sort of quarry. This person they were after would already be on the move and looking for a hole... a hiding place. Sanctuary.

Even though there would be a good number of people in the field, it was a huge area in rough country, and a single experienced man who didn't want to be found, likely wouldn't be found. Charlie had seen Indian fugitives roam this country for weeks, even months without being apprehended. Though if the crime was not too serious, some of them might eventually come in on their own, tired of the hard way they were living. Even a few white men, survivalists mostly, had lasted a long time out there. Some, of course, had never been found— suicides probably—men who could not bear to give up or give in. The older and wiser of the authorities knew all this but figured the public expected them to keep the pressure on for as long as possible... and too, they *might* get lucky. But this time, of course, they had no idea who they were dealing with.

Thomas took a different view and thought the three of *them* might very well have a shot at this guy. He had been on the run himself and had a pretty good handle on what such a person might be thinking. The authorities, on the other hand, seldom apprehended anyone in this country without a little help from the locals, most of whom were not inclined to volunteer information to the law, preferring instead to handle things their own way.

Harley Ponyboy, now with the added support of clan, felt reassured. His "grandmother" had suffered a great hurt and thus, so had he. It was personal now. Clan ties come with deep roots, even among the more modern thinking Navajo. Sometimes this led to vendettas that might entail all manner of evil, witches and worse, and sometimes with far-reaching effects.

It was nearly noon when they ran across the first of the advancing phalanx of searchers, spread out like an old-time rabbit drive, and headed in altogether the wrong direction.

Thomas waited as the end volunteer drew near. "How's it going, my man?"

Sweat streaked the young searcher's face, and he carried his jacket tied around his waist. He stopped and regarded Thomas's horse with a wistful expression. He was Navajo, and by the look of him would have preferred to be somewhere else. "Beats me, brother. You got any water?" He shook his empty canteen. "Goes fast out here afoot." Then smiled at the fat canteen on the horse's saddle.

Thomas untied the water and passed it to him. "Any word on your guy's location or where he might be headed?"

"Reports have him all over the place." The young man took a deep swallow from the canteen and passed it back. "People that live out here are starting to see boogers everywhere. There are so many volunteers they've got the dogs running in circles. I'm going to give it another hour and then head back to the truck. I doubt they'll have this many show up tomorrow." He grinned. "You wouldn't want to sell that horse, would you?"

Thomas looped the canteen over the horn and chuckled. "Not today." He scanned the horizon. "Well, we're supposed to be out here looking for cows. We'll let someone know should we spot anything suspicious."

The young man waved over his shoulder and hitched up his jacket, which was now nearly dragging the ground.

Thomas turned to Charlie, who had remained silent during the short exchange. "About what I thought. Our guy is up high and gone to ground. He won't peek his head out until this posse is back at the saloon."

Harley sniffed. "They had to cross his sign up on that ridge. These boys couldn't find a piss-ant in a sugar bowl."

Charlie shook his head and smiled at Harley, looked to the high country and agreed with Thomas. "He's up *there* somewhere—laughing at us. We need to get above him... and then just wait him out."

# 8

## *Tressa*

Luca scratched himself, lolled back against his pack, and peered through the stunted growth at the entrance to the little cave-like shelter. He was totally at ease, though it was above eight thousand feet and had been cold the previous night. Once again, he was grateful for the sleeping bag. Reaching behind him, he pulled the little binoculars from the side pocket of the pack and spent a few minutes sweeping the slope almost two miles below. Too far to pick up a man on foot probably, but should one have a steady enough hand, it would be close enough to see one on horseback. He saw nothing for the moment but knew that somewhere there were three very determined and not unskilled followers—not part of the general melee that had broken out everywhere this morning. These other three were from before and slowly, methodically, tracking him. Twice now he had fallen back and watched them, close enough to know they were *Indios*. They were well mounted and moved with an assurance that rankled him. Eventually, however, those horses would prove more of a hindrance than an asset—it was still another thousand feet to the summit and would only get rougher. Many of those volunteers would eventually give up and go home, but not these three; they were in it for the long haul and like him, apparently had some skin in the game.

There was a plastic water bottle hanging from the pack. He had already filled it a couple of times from springs and seeps, but still it would not be enough should one consider the packets of dried food he had left to fix. His bad arm was improving rapidly; he guessed the nerves might finally be recovering from the shock suffered in the wreck. In any case he now had some use of the arm, and that was a great help in this rough country.

That first night, after the girl, he had stopped to grill strips of lamb in the lee of a cliff and despite the wind-driven grit, found it delicious and hoped the rest of the back-strap would keep until he could once again risk a fire. *It was fresh meat that was helping his arm,* he was sure. It was cool up here even in the daytime, and he hoped what he had left of the lamb would stay good for a while yet. If not, he would have to cut it into thin strips and hang them to dry. There was a tiny little seep at the back of the declivity, and if he dug it out just a little, made a basin in the mud, he thought it might make enough water to get along. You had to walk right up to this hiding place to find it, and he felt very fortu-nate that he had noticed it at all. A man might stay safely hidden here a good long time… were it not for those three trackers. There was a growing resentment in him toward the three, and he began to have bad thoughts about them. He exercised even more caution in regard to the sign he left behind, thinking to slow their progress even more.

There was no urgent need to be on his way north and while he didn't waver in that eventuality, he was a man of extraordinary perseverance—well tutored in the value of patience—he could wait.

Long ago in Sonora he had killed a very important man, for pay, and had to stay out over three months living off the land alone, and a sparse land at that. The *Federales* had brought in the most feared of government trackers, *Yaquis,* from northern Chihuahua. They were men to reckon with, and finally he had to kill two of them, before the others quit and went home. They probably wouldn't have quit even then if he had not eaten part of one as a warning. Even *Yaquis* have their limit. He would discourage these *Indios del Norte* one way or another. Everyone has their limit.

He wished now that he had lain in wait for one of those outlying searchers, one with a rifle. Guns were hard to come by where he was from, and he had never developed any particular skill with one; but he did know how to shoot. The important thing with a gun was to have the *cojones* to instantly, and without thinking about it, be willing to kill a man—anything less made it a liability. Hesitation was what got you hurt in his opinion. He maintained that guns might even be a hindrance for a man of his skills; yet, where these long ranges were involved, it might be handy to have one. He had stealthily passed by several herders' camps before dawn that morning, knowing they would have dogs to alert them, and probably a gun of some sort handy. Once things settled down, he would venture forth at night and see what could be done. It was all just a matter of time.

As he rested himself in his little sanctuary, his thoughts turned to Tressa and their lives in the little village in Mexico. How far away those days now seemed. It was hardly believable that their life had been so simple. It was difficult, yes, but little ever changed in that village. Should one grow up there and know his limits, there was very little stress involved, and the days melted away like butter... until Tressa decided it wasn't good enough, and began pushing him to do better. First it was just a pair of new shoes, then a store-bought dress, and finally then... a better house. "Luca, do you not see what the Baca's have done with their *casita*? Why shouldn't we have such as that? Surely a man of your abilities should be able to provide as well as old man Baca, who only runs a few goats for a living. Maybe if you found a job on the fishing boats over on the Baja?" She pouted and fussed, and coiled her hair around one finger and tugged at it. "Elsa Sanchez and her new husband went to Puerto Penasco, and now he is gutting fish for the *turistas* down on the docks. He only works four or five hours in the afternoon, when the boats come in, no more than that, and already he is making three times what he made here in the village, and that for six days a week hard labor." She smiled out the window as though she could see all the way to Puerto Penasco, "You should see their new house, Luca. He and his cousins built it—with an inside toilet no less." Here the credibility of the thing was stretched to the limit, and secretly she wondered if Elsa Sanchez had lied to her mother about the toilet. No one here in the village had such a convenience, and most would not know how to operate it if they did. Tressa's voice became even more petulant, "All I know is that *I* am the one to deserve so fine a thing as that. Elsa Sanchez don't know her ass from a hole in the ground anyway." The inequity of it brought a tear, and it was all she could do not to weep outright at her misfortune.

"What?" Luca had said, "Move away from our place here, where we were born, and go to strangers in a strange place to find our living? I don't think so, Tressa. Making adobes was good enough for my father, and he had six children to feed. We have none and only feed ourselves. This is good enough."

But Tressa was young, quite good looking in a provincial sort of way, and she was attracted to that life she saw, on the rare occasions they took the bus to Hermosillo. She harped so insistently and grew so unpleasant that finally he relented and they moved to Guaymas, where she had cousins who she said might help them get a new start. Work, though, was scarce, and eventually their situation became desperate, and this caused Luca to be drawn into a very different life indeed.

He became an "enforcer" for a local group involved in all sorts of dubious enterprises. It was a business he knew little about, other than it required certain people to be beaten, and sometimes, worse. He had always been good at beating people up and had been the scourge of the village children and later the young rakes who hung out at the *cantina*. Happily, this job required little previous experience, at least in the more serious requirements of the position, and from the beginning it seemed to be in the natural order of things and what he had been meant to do. After only a few months, he conceded, and admitted to Tressa she had been right all along, and this *was* an easier, more enjoyable way to live.

Tressa only sniffed and said, "I tol' you so. We were wasting our lives in that little hole of a village. Now you are making good money, and we have a chance to be someone."

In any case, it was all the same to him, and if the money made Tressa happy, he didn't mind the work. He did occasionally have to go to jail for some little something, assault, or perhaps petty larceny, things that were part of his new job description and not considered particularly bad in their new neighborhood. One did what one must to get along—everyone there knew that.

In these short stints in jail he became more educated, particularly in things that came in handy in his new line of work, and before long he rose in his profession to the point he attracted attention from people outside the local organization, bigger people, who offered more challenging jobs and paid more money. Luca might be considered by some to be an ignorant person, but too many confused ignorance with stupidity, and these people later paid the consequences of their misconception.

Eventually, Tressa put away quite a little savings from Luca's work and looked forward to a new house and an even more comfortable life, perhaps hiring a girl to help out and allow *her* a bit more freedom... though freedom to do what, she would not say. It was just then, when things were going so well, that he had been arrested, and this time on more serious charges, charges that would most certainly entail a lengthy prison sentence, causing Tressa to think it might be a good time to disassociate herself from him entirely. Suddenly, even the people he worked for... no longer knew him.

It happened that there were two Americans in jail, newly arrived and in bad need of protection. They prevailed upon Luca to help them out, and in return they shared with him the little money they received from relatives in the states, and in the idleness of their days, attempted to teach Luca English. Although it was in the redneck vernacular of their kind, Luca thought it something that would impress Tressa. And once his curiosity was aroused, he applied himself to the utmost of his ability. He repeated for Tressa the many stories the gringos had whiled away the hours telling him. These stories of America so lit a fire in Tressa that she no longer missed a single visiting day, as once she had done. She couldn't get enough of how things were in the *Ustados Unidos*.

Mexico employs Napoleonic Law; meaning one must prove himself innocent, instead of the other way around, and for Luca this proved problematic—in the end impossible. The lawyer Tressa had retained for him was young and a drunkard and came to him admitting he had no chance in court, advising Luca to just plead guilty and take the less severe consequences. Luca was assured the judge would go easier on him and he would not be gone so long this way.

It was not long after that Tressa quit coming to the jail, and word drifted back to him that she had disappeared, and to heap insult upon injury, with Luca's own lawyer who, as it should turn out, had relatives in the United States. The lawyer required only a certain amount of money, he told Tressa, to get them both out of Mexico and to the promised-land—complete with green cards. They could make themselves a handsome living performing *musica* and the *baile* in his family's bar. He told her the *guittara* was his real talent and that he could sing a bird off a limb. He would, of course, pay her back the expense involved—once they were established, and the money started coming in. He failed to mention that her part of *performing* would be waiting tables and eventually more base duties, should the opportunity present itself.

Poor Tressa eventually found herself in even more dreadful circumstances than in the little village where they grew up.

Luca, truly alone now, finally had to approach his own family to engineer his release, though certainly they would have much preferred he remain where he was forever. It was not really an *escape* nor was it so much a *release* but rather a combination of the two, brought about through money and the endemic corruption of the system. He didn't blame Tressa so much for all this, as she was young and not fully accountable in his eyes. The man she ran off with, however, *would* pay, of that he was certain. It only remained for him to find a way to the U.S., where he might find her and make things right between them. She had written him one last letter to the prison and by some miracle he had received it, though without the ten dollars she had sent as a peace offering. The letter had a return address for him to answer back and possibly tell her that he had forgiven her. Tressa had no idea he might one day actually show up in a place so far away. She had not thought him that clever. She herself would probably not have made it to the U.S. had it not been for the lawyer turned musician, and even *he* had finally lost interest, leaving poor Tressa pretty much to her own devises.

Luca had harmed no one on leaving his incarceration, which was part of the deal his uncles had made, and in fact he had intended to harm no one on this entire journey, should things have played out as planned. Now, of course, it was different. It was a slippery slope when once one lost his footing.

# 9

## The Chase

Thomas and Charlie left their horses tied to a sparsely limbed juniper. They had let the horses graze only a few hours the night before as they didn't trust them to the gunny-sack hobbles they had made.

Harley, on the other hand, had left his mule, Shorty, loose all night, knowing it wouldn't leave its companions. Even though Shorty was much smarter than either of the two horses, he had been raised by a mare, and for all equine social commitments considered *himself* a horse as well. While mules have many sterling qualities, they do have a few less endearing attributes as well, one of which is braying unpredictably and without any discernable reason. They get this from their donkey sires, and it is, unfortunately, an uncontrollable urge. It's not the more refined neighing of the horse, mind you, a sound which might be carried away by any small wind, but rather a raucous, mind numbing blast that could carry, literally, for miles across open country. And that is why Harley and Shorty had been sent to search out a camp where he might obtain more food and possibly, if a clan member could be found, even the loan of a rifle and a few cartridges. It would be best that Shorty be far from the more delicate sunrise scouting mission.

A rifle was something Charlie should have thought of before they left home. He might even have stopped at his Aunt Annie's place and borrowed one of her late husband's guns. He had been quite the hunter and owned several different calibers. He'd kept plenty of ammunition too, if Clyde hadn't shot it all up. Clyde liked to shoot, though like Charlie, he was a poor shot by any measure. Who could have known this venture would evolve into this. It had been intended as a daytrip to satisfy their curiosity, not the marathon it was turning out to be. He would have done things differently had he known how this little jaunt would play out.

Thomas led the way up the side of the ridge, staying low to the ground and taking what advantage of the terrain he could. Charlie followed and deferred to Thomas's natural talent in the business. Since coming back from university, he had already learned a great deal from Thomas and was sometimes surprised to see how little of what he once thought he knew was of value out here. There was education… and then there was *education*, and he was finding one was often very different from the other. Thomas's brand of education sometimes proved to be the more practical, even in Charlie's more civilized line of work. He was still glad he had decided on the university and was proud of his accomplishments there, but now and then felt more than a little regret at missing out on certain aspects of a more traditional learning process. Harley and Thomas were self-sufficient in this country, and he was coming to the conclusion that it entitled them to a certain respect in that regard. It was in Charlie to learn these things too, and in time he would, but for now, out here, he must often defer to their judgment.

They crept their way to the top of the ridge, carefully adjusting their course to follow a screen of stunted underbrush interspersed with cedar and pinion pine.

Thomas spent a good ten minutes glassing the upper rim of the bluff below Pastora Peak, then passed the glasses. "There must be dozens of good hiding places along that one rim alone." He ran his tongue along his front teeth. "It's no damn wonder the law never catches anyone out here. Too big a country, that's all."

Charlie looked through the binoculars for only a minute or so before handing them back. "Harley said his tracks were headed this way, and there's no better cover above that rim that I can see. I suspect he's right up there somewhere."

Thomas nodded. "He'll come loose by and by, I'm sure, but it could be awhile." He hesitated. "We could always go back and report where we *think* he is and then go on home." Thomas was thinking of his children and Lucy taking care of their sheep, and of old Paul T'Sosi, as he grew less able to help out in his old age.

Charlie narrowed his eyes at the rim. "No, they have plenty of *supposed* sightings already. I doubt they would attach much importance to ours—he'd get away, and go on doing what he's doing. We need to stop him now, if we can." He needs to pay his debt here *first*." He turned his head and looked back the way they had come. "We're not going home till it's over."

~~~~~~~~~

Harley poked at the fire and handed out cold fry-bread to be warmed on sticks, and stirred the skillet of bacon with his knife. He had gathered quite a haul down in the camps, and all three watched greedily as the meat sizzled and popped in the pan. There would be enough for several more days, should they be frugal, but frugality would only come later, when they were again running out of provisions. The evening breeze was flowing down the mountain and would carry the smoke and smell of bacon down country. They were well hidden in a deep gully that opened up to a little grass-filled bottom, and their stock had been turned loose, one at a time, to graze. They knew better than to turn loose more than one, as two might form a conspiracy and quit the camp.

Thomas stared into the fire. "We'll have to leave the horses if we're going higher. They'll be all right down here if we hobble them. There's plenty of grass for a few days and water too, in those potholes under the bank... no need for them to go anywhere. I think they'll be good here."

Harley turned to see Shorty standing behind him. It was the mule's turn to be loose, and he could smell fry-bread and thought he might get a bite if Harley was in a generous mood; if not he would grab Harley's straw hat off his head and pitch it up in the air. That usually worked when nothing else would. Harley would chuckle. His sister used to do that same thing when they were little. Shorty reminded him of her in a lot of ways. His sister was dead now, and he tried not to recall what she looked like.

"Shorty can travel in that kind of hobbles if he takes a mind." Harley said this and considered various alternatives as he gauged the mule's small feet, and finally just passed him a bit of fry-bread. "I guess I'll have to side-hobble him––he won' be able to go far that way." The mule, satisfied with the trifling bribe, backed out of the firelight and returned to the horses with a smug look. Harley smiled after him. He'd had Shorty nearly twenty years, since they were both youngsters in fact, and hoped he might last another fifteen or twenty, not out of the question for a mule. It had something to do with hybrid vigor, he'd heard.

The next morning the three rose before dawn and returned on foot to the lookout spot of the day before. They made themselves comfortable and prepared to wait. Harley thought the first rays of the sun on the butte might make something more discernable. A different slant of light could make all the difference, he said.

As the first rays of the sun spilled over the rim, Charlie looked over at the other two. "You don't think Shorty will start bellowing and give us away, do you?" Even Charlie knew burros and mules liked to meet the sun with their own particular greeting, though he thought Shorty might be out of range, what with a brisk wind being in their favor.

Harley didn't take his eyes off the rim, his gaze locked on just a shadow halfway up a broken rock outcrop. "…I don' guess that matters now… *he* knows we're here."

Thomas shifted the glasses in that direction while Charlie strained his eyes for a glimpse of something out of place.

Thomas nudged him and passed the glasses. "Yep, he knows." They hadn't foreseen this turn of events.

Charlie studied the rim but still wouldn't have spotted it if Thomas hadn't finally pointed a finger. Just the hint of a shadow in the rock, nothing at all, invisible, if not for the little strip of clothe fluttering almost imperceptibly in the breeze.

"He hasn't been there since last night, I guess." Harley gathered up his water bottle and peered toward their own camp, still enveloped in shadow. "He prob'ly left early last night, so he's been gone awhile. We could climb up there and have a look… but that's what he wants us to do. That's why he left that little flag."

Thomas agreed with a meaningful nod toward the hidden retreat. "Probably has a little rockslide engineered, or if he has a gun, he's maybe laying for us… but that's not likely, I guess… He woulda already shot us if he had a gun."

"So where do you think he's headed?" Charlie's mind was awhirl as he puzzled through information so clearly evident to the others.

"I've got a pretty good idea." Thomas scooped up his own gear and was right behind Harley, leaving Charlie to work his mind around it all.

It took over an hour to reach camp, and Charlie, even after catching up, had a hard time keeping up. The little clearing was already bathed in sunlight, and the warm fragrant smell of pine washed over the camp like a balm. Shorty lay not twenty feet from where Harley had last seen him, throat cut with one clean slash across the jugular. One hindquarter had been laid open and meat stripped away.

Most of their food had been taken, and what was left was piled in a small mound, opened, and urinated on. The two horses were missing, though the saddles were there, for what little good it would do anyone. The chinches and latigos had been cut to pieces.

Harley walked slowly over to Shorty and silently, gently, reached down and touched one long ear. No Navajo did this, nor *any* kind of person he was familiar with. Sam Shorthair had been right—this was a *mojado*, a *chólló*, a throwback to the ancient and fierce tribes of Mexico.

Charlie, unnerved, stared at the mule, recalling a lecture by a noted anthropologist. *All men are capable of all things. The cortex of the human brain comes preprogramed, and even today primitive responses can be triggered by the proper stimuli.* Charlie could see truth in those words now and wondered at the disparity in the amount of stimuli required of certain individuals to commit those most heinous of acts.

Thomas hardly looked at Shorty as he moved past to find what had befallen the horses. The intruder had not wanted the horses, otherwise they would be missing a saddle, and that meant he had no intention of making a run for it. No, this person was confident in his ability to elude his pursuers and whoever else might have an interest in him. The mule was just a warning. Again, the feeling washed over him that they were not dealing with a man at all, but something much more powerful, and the word *Yeenaaldiooshii* again played across his mind, causing him to tremble, and a shiver, fear perhaps, passed over him like an icy wind.

The horses hadn't gone far and he found them calmly grazing a little patch of grass in the pines, and though they were still hobbled, the hair was worn off around their fetlocks. They had probably panicked and bolted at the violent death of the mule and smell of fresh blood. A horse, hobbled by the front feet, still can travel a good distance, and at a remarkable speed when properly motivated. Thomas cut the now stiff burlap hobbles off the horses and let them drift on down toward the flats, where he knew they would fall in with one of the other bunches let loose to roam by area stockmen. It's common for reservation horses to mingle freely with those of others, and owners only come for them when needed; usually someone will know where any particular little bunch is ranging.

Thomas knew that in order to keep up with their quarry, they would now have to travel on foot, and just as fast and light if there was to be any chance of success. Mules can go where horses can't, and that is why Shorty had been chosen. This person knew his business... if indeed he was a person.

When Thomas arrived back at camp, the other two had salvaged very little beyond their blankets, which reeked of urine, and a small store of bacon Harley had hung in a distant spruce in case of bears. They also had what little food they had taken with them that morning in their jacket pockets, but unless they ran across another *hogan* or camp, the pickings would be lean. They would have to be as tough as the man they followed and in the end... maybe even tougher

Thomas saw Harley standing over the mule and watched as his friend opened his knife and began cutting meat from the partially skinned hindquarter. Harley understood what they were up against and didn't let sentiment stand in his way. Charley grimaced but said nothing as he stacked the saddles back under some overhanging brush and piled dead branches in front of them. They would come back for them when their business was finished. Not a single word had been spoken among the three since they entered the camp, and silently they left it now to the jays, and magpies and other wild things.

By early afternoon Harley thought they might actually be losing ground to the killer. "This guy is like a machine— he don' stop, he don' rest, and he eats and drinks on the go."

Harley had found little sign of the man when leaving their camp and now admitted it was as though he had flown away like a bird... or a witch. Eventually he realized the man had wrapped his feet in the burlap bags their food donations had come in. It made him near impossible to follow on that hard ground. "It don' matter none," he muttered, "I got a bead on where he's heading." Harley had taken on a grim determination that could be seen in his eyes and the set of his jaw. This was not the carefree Harley the other two had come to know.

"He's only got about an hour or two on us, at most," Thomas calculated, hitching up his Levi's and shaking his head at the sky. The wispy "mare's tail" clouds were harbingers of a weather front. In this season it would probably bring rain out of Mexico along with it—there would be the clean, fresh smell of wet mesquite running before it. The sign of this *challó*, as Harley now called him, could disappear altogether should they get another downpour.

By mid-morning all three of the men were sweating, and though they carried little in the way of gear, they were breathing hard, and Charlie wondered how long they could maintain such a pace. Already the muscles of his calves were trying to spasm.

Thomas had moved out in front, and as they topped yet another interminable ridge, he swept the broken country beyond through slitted eyes. Well in the distance he could just make out what appeared to be a "summer" *hogan*. There had been a time in his people's past when these brush shelters had been their only protection. Sometimes they might be covered with hides but only in the fiercest of weather. They had lived much like the Utes in those days and, like their cousins the Apache, in the not so distant past. The more traditional *Diné* still favored them, conditions permitting.

While Thomas didn't like the idea, Harley thought they should alter course to check out the dwelling, see if there might be a chance of adding to their meager supplies or maybe borrow a gun, which he had not been able to accomplish on his last foraging venture. He wanted a long gun. Charlie agreed with Harley, but Thomas allowed he would stay on the *mojado's* trail, and they could just catch up with him if they were able. Privately, Charlie thought this foolish, but knowing Thomas's stubborn nature thought it pointless to argue. The two men stood for a moment, staring at one another, each hoping the other might relent. Finally Charlie pulled his .38 from its shoulder holster, and for a moment Harley thought he meant to shoot their friend.

Charlie passed the gun across to Thomas with a grim smile. "I guess you may as well take this then." Though the gun was loaded, he reached in his pocket to produce another four or five grimy cartridges. "Try not to put yourself in the position of having to use this. If you run across this guy, just back off until we catch up before you do anything crazy—try using a little discretion for a change." Charlie meant it too.

Thomas smiled and nodded. "Anything you say, college boy. You know me."

While Charlie pulled off the shoulder holster and passed it over, Harley stood contemplating the pair. He had known Thomas a long time, and if discretion meant what he thought it meant, he knew it wasn't his friend's long suit.

As the two of them watched Thomas move off through the scrub oak, Charlie felt it was a mistake to let him go on alone but could see the man would have it no other way. Thomas had the gun now and most of the food; he should be okay if he didn't let his temper cause him to do something rash.

Harley watched as Thomas disappeared in the under-brush. "Do you think I should go with him?"

"No, you're the one to talk to these people up here—if we are lucky, they will be clansmen of yours and willing to help us more than most. The old woman said there were lots of Reed People up here. Maybe these will be some of them."

As they drew closer to the brush arbor, Harley held up a hand for Charlie to stop and then studied the place from the shade of a larger than usual scrub oak. There was no one about that he could see, but that would not be unusual for this time of day. The herder would be off with the stock. It was then he saw a slight movement at the back of the shelter and motioned Charlie forward with him. *Maybe it's a dog,* he thought, *but no, if it was a dog, it would be out here raising a ruckus... if not trying to eat us alive.* It was a Navajo dog's job to raise an alarm; it had been their major purpose for thousands of years, and they knew their job.

Charlie moved up alongside him, and Harley pointed to where he thought he had seen some sort of movement. There was nothing either of them could see now, still Harley hesitated, waiting, watching. He was almost ready to move forward when he heard a small noise, a whine, or tiny yelp... something.

Charlie motioned for them to split up and move to either side of the shelter. He almost wished he had kept the gun now and moved forward with the sense that he might soon be sorry he didn't.

Harley reached the side of the shelter first and peered inside through the loosely woven wall of the structure. Charlie was at the open front, and Harley didn't have time to warn him as a flash of brown lunged against the end of a chain and growled low in its throat. Fortunately for Charlie the chain was such that it ended just short of the opening, and the big female could not quite reach him.

Harley moved to the entrance, considered the dog, and then grinned at the look on Charlie's face. "You are lucky that dog didn't get you. She's got pups back there in a box. That's why she didn't bark right off—didn't want to give them away unless she had to—they're just like coyotes that way. The owner probably has another dog out herding with him. Those pups aren't weaned, so he left the female with them."

Harley spoke softly to the dog in Navajo, and after a while she calmed down and let him approach and even ruffle the hair on her back. Harley had a way with dogs, and Charlie doubted he could have done the same. It was something in the way Harley spoke old-time Navajo or maybe the smell of him… something told the dog he was okay. Charley was finally able to edge past and have a look around. One pup was a blue merle color, and the other black and white, giving testament to their mixed heritage.

It was not considered good manners for a stranger to enter even so loosely built a brush shelter as this one uninvited, but in this instance there were extenuating circumstances, and allowances would have to be made. The people who lived here might not be aware of the danger now stalking the area and should be warned, but time was short and they needed to catch up with Thomas. The person that lived here had already been lucky. If Harley had spotted this place so had the man they were following. Only the fact that they were close behind may have prevented him from doing more harm here. Harley called from the front yard, "I think we've got company. Someone's coming, and they're in a hurry."

Charlie once again squeezed past the chained dog, which lowered her ears and gave him the stock-dog stare, one that would stop a sheep dead in its tracks. He reached Harley's side just as a rider came into view from the east, and the two of them stood watching as the horseman quickly closed the gap. He was young and carried a .22 rifle across his saddle. He waited till he was nearly upon them before pulling his horse to an abrupt stop, scattering dirt and small rocks over their feet. This was the way young men were these days, Harley thought—no consideration.

Harley looked down at his boots and frowned before raising his eyes to the young man. "*Eh t'eeh*, Cousin. Where from?"

The boy, Billy Zahnii, in his twenties, seemed suspicious of Harley's old-time use of a language which he himself had only a partial understanding. He stared the two up and down and then looked around and beyond them, as though to confirm they were alone. He said nothing and kept the rifle in front of him. It was an old Winchester pump action with an octagon barrel. Charlie's grandfather had one just like it when Charlie was a boy. He had used it many times to pot a rabbit or ground squirrel. They were fine rifles in their day, and the thought crossed his mind he should ask Annie what had happened to it… maybe get it for his son.

Everyone was silent for an embarrassing amount of time, and then the boy, seeing the other two were not intimidated, said, "I'm coming from our band of sheep down on "Water Springs Up"—about two miles from here. What are you people doing out here on foot? You don't look like part of the search parties."

Harley thought the boy rude and was about to say as much. But Charlie answered first. "We're not with them, but I'm glad you know what's going on. The man they are looking for passed by your camp this morning. It was a good thing you were already gone with the sheep. He's a dangerous person and might have hurt someone here if he got the chance… He doesn't need much of a reason to hurt people." He pulled his badge out of his pocket and held it out for the young man to see: NAVAJO NATION LEGAL SERVICES. "We've been after this guy for several days now." This seemed to mollify the boy to some degree, and he relaxed, even lowered the muzzle of his rifle a bit.

Harley spoke now, first in Navajo, and then seeing the boy wasn't connecting, switched to English. "Are you out here alone, little brother?" At this boy's age he himself often had to spend weeks alone with the sheep up in Tsé Bii' Ndzigail, Monument Valley, where his people still lived.

The boy sniffed. "I only work for these people who own the sheep. This is Delbert Natanii's camp. They've gone to town for groceries, most likely won't be back here till evening." The young man straightened himself in the saddle. "They own a lot of sheep and run two camps up here in the summer. They have to drop off supplies up above first, then they will circle back down here on the road."

Charlie shot the boy a sharp glance. "You mean farther up under the rim and on around the mountain?" There was an urgency there that took the boy by surprise.

"...Uh, yes, over there." He indicated Pastora Peak with a push of his chin. My uncle and younger brother are up there." And then he said, "Why!"

Harley looked in the direction the boy had pointed. "Can you get a horse up to their camp from here?"

"Naah. You would have to come in from the other side if you were horseback. My uncle or brother will have to ride down from that camp and pick up their groceries from the truck on the other side of the mountain and then pack them up to their camp. There's no road up there." Worry was becoming evident in the boy's voice, and he looked from one to the other of the two as if deciding once and for all if he could trust them. "You think this crazy person is headed that way, do you?"

"The sign points to that, yes, and I'm not going to tell you otherwise. But this guy has food enough already and may not bother your people at all. We're pushing him pretty hard, and he may just go ta ground again—hide until he sees a way out." Harley wanted the boy to know the situation just as it was. After all, his life could depend on it.

Charlie interrupted, "Right now *we* need food." And looking the boy in the eye asked, "Do you have any other gun than that .22. Something bigger?"

The boy thought only a moment before deciding and said, "We have an old 30-40 Krag in there under my bedding. We hardly ever take it out unless we see bear sign around." He thought again. "...Probably only have a handful of shells for it. It kicks like a mule and is too heavy to carry around all the time. I don't like it myself, but it shoots straight." And then he said, "I can come with you!"

Charlie shook his head. "No, we already have one man up there on his trail. We'll catch up to him by evening, if we hurry. We don't need any more help other than some food...

whatever you have will do… and that rifle." He again saw a shadow of doubt cross the boy's features. "I'll personally see that it gets back to you, and we can pay you for whatever food we take. I don't suppose you are a Reed People, are you?"

"No, I'm of the Red Clays and born for the *Bit'ahnii*. The owner of this camp is a Reed People."

Charlie blinked. "I'm *Bit'ahnii*, and Harley here is of the Reed People, so we are related, all of us, family… We will treat you right."

Upon hearing this, the boy slowly nodded and headed inside, where he retrieved the old military rifle and whatever cartridges there were, then began collecting food. It was more than the two had hoped, and they took it with many thanks.

"Well," Harley said taking the bag of food, "we are falling behind and need ta be on our way. Thank the owner of this place for us. Let him know that it is family that has his gun. He can ask his clan sister, She Has Horses, the old woman down below whose granddaughter was killed. Maybe it will be one of these very bullets that settles that score." This was more than Harley was used to saying at one time, and he seemed pleased when the boy acknowledged it with a grim smile and waved away their offer to pay for the food. He stood waving goodbye till they were nearly out of sight.

~~~~~

Thomas Begay did not stop till he was at the base of the bluff and could see no apparent way to go higher without continuing around the mountain, and even then he wasn't sure what he would find. Anyone who hunts knows the secret is to stay above the game—hunting up into the quarry puts a pursuer at a disadvantage, and a dangerous one too, should the game be man.

Thomas had expended a lot of energy in the climb and rested now in the shade of the bluff as he caught his breath and gazed across distant panoramas of mountain and desert.

In the old days, and on a clear day, it was said a man up high could see as far as 75 miles in this country, sometimes more. That was before the coal-fired generating plants began operating. Now one was lucky to see a third that far no matter how high the vantage. Still, it was magnificent. Some think the *Diné* indifferent to the more esthetic nuances of their homeland but when taken from it they, almost without exception, miss it deep in their soul and their *hozoji* suffers to one degree or another. An illness of the heart sometimes ensues, and has been the cause of many a one going "back to the blanket." Thomas thought about Charlie Yazzie and wondered if this might not be what brought him back to the reservation, when clearly he had the ability and education to be a success most anywhere. Even though Charlie sometimes disavowed any traditional cultural ties, Thomas got the feeling there was more to his return than just the job at Legal Services. Originally the young lawyer had applied for a spot on the legal team, but when one finally did open up, he turned it down in favor of the job he was doing now—a job that took him out amongst the people and to the far reaches of the reservation. He had pretty much carved out his own niche in the tribal hierarchy and had helped many a one who had no one else to turn to, including Thomas himself.

Thomas Begay studied his back trail for some sign of the other two. He was sure they could not be far behind, but should something delay them, they might choose to wait until morning rather than attempt the final climb in poor light. The ground was hard, mostly rock and shale, and he could find no sign of the quarry, causing him to wonder if Harley Ponyboy might have been wrong in thinking the fugitive had come this way at all. For all they knew he might have circled back below them and already be headed out to a road. To some that might seem a foolish plan, what with all the searchers in the area, but this was not your average sort of renegade; this one went well beyond what some might think. Harley and Thomas both were convinced he had powers.

And even if he didn't, and Charlie Yazzie was right, Thomas Begay knew this was a dangerous man, skilled at what he did, and an adversary to be reckoned with. While Thomas was a man confident in his own abilities he still was apprehensive and had his doubts about taking on such a person and thus his resolve weakened as the day wore on. There was no turning back now, however, the game was in play and there was nothing for it but to persevere and hope when the time came he would measure up to the task.

He thought of Lucy Tallwoman and his children who were now out of school and while the two of them could at least provide a bit of help to their adopted mother and grandfather it would not be the same as him being there. His place was there not here he thought *those sheep need shearing and Annie Eagletree's cattle are still to be gathered There are plenty of other things I should be doing rather than running around the country looking for some wild man.*

~~~~~~~

# 10

## *The Devil*

Luca had found himself yet another hiding place, and while this one had no water, he doubted he would be there long enough for it to matter. The three trackers were pushing him, and showed no signs of giving up. He had hoped the destruction of their camp would dissuade, or at least discourage them, but apparently it had quite the opposite effect. When he thought about it, he probably would have been much the same himself, but then not many were as dedicated to their work as Luca Tarango, certainly not these *Norteños*, who he doubted had it in them to confront a truly bad man. Even some who thought themselves bad men had no concept of what one actually was. Down in *Mexicó* there still were "bad men" of the fiercest kind... and he knew for certain he was one of them.

He thought of the time in San Carlos, when coming out of a bar, he was spotted by members of another gang and recognized as working for the rival faction. The two ringleaders were determined to make an example of him and, at the same time, impress their two new recruits. They had beaten him then—they had guns, and he thought it prudent not to fight back, and rightly so. That would have been sure death. Only in the movies does one man do well against four able adversaries. He knew the best he could hope for would be for them to beat him senseless and possibly leave him for dead... All he had to do was endure.

These were practiced people and not easy to fool, but he had the inner strength of his *indigene* forebears, taking the beating without a whimper and withstanding the thin-bladed knife, gently probing, determined to detect the slightest sign of awareness. Fortunately for Luca, more people began coming out of the bar, and in the end his attackers did leave him for dead, and he was nearly so. It was as though his mind completely disconnected from his body, drifted above it, and knew no pain or suffering of worldly flesh. No one tried to interfere or help him, as that would have been foolish. He lay in the gutter with his cheek tight against the curb until his mind returned from wherever it had gone to hide. There was a smile on his broken lips as he crawled his way to the nearby alley, where the next morning a cleaning woman found him and did what she could, and then called the number he whispered. It was nearly a month before he was, in any way, his former self. He'd had plenty of time to think and knew finally that it was time to do what had to be done. Letting something like this pass without consequence would be the end of a person in his line of work.

While not a religious man, in any sense of the word, he kept a cross on the wall above their bed and even hung a rosary from it as added insurance. He and Tressa went to mass occasionally... but he never went to confession. He did not trust the priests so far as that. Even during the beating he had not called upon God to help him as he felt it would be taken as a sign of weakness and possibly cause the punishment to become even more severe. It was in the nature of these people to test a man's faith and prove it unfounded if they could. This was as much for their own peace of mind as anything else.

Two of his assailants he had recognized, and even knew where they lived; they were brothers and had been the lesser of the four who beat him. These new recruits had only kicked him a few times, hung back during the worst of the beating, and did not participate in the later knife work. These two he only killed and did not exact any particular satisfaction from it. They were young and only doing what was expected of them; he understood that. It was their job, and he would have done the same.

While he had not previously known the identities of the two in charge, he did by the time he had finished with the brothers. The second and youngest brother talked, though he knew by then it wouldn't save his life; that was no longer his goal. To his way of thinking, it was the older two that brought him and his brother to this end, and he felt it only right they should suffer the same fate. It was true the brothers were not nearly such bad men as those other two... but of course, in time, they would have been.

When Luca caught the third man, he was coming out of his girlfriend's shabby apartment in a bad part of town. The man had become cautious after hearing the fate of the two brothers but still didn't connect their deaths with the beating of Luca Tarango. It never entered his mind that so insignificant a person could have survived such abuse, let alone have the audacity to seek revenge. *Those brothers probably ran afoul of a rival gang, or perhaps angered higher ups in their own organization. Not unusual, but I would have thought I would hear something about it.* This is what he was thinking as he stepped past a doorway and felt the garrote around his neck, but only for a few moments, then he felt absolutely nothing. Luca let him return to consciousness several times before showing him the final mercy of death.

No, Luca's main focus was the man with the knife. He was the one who made the added effort to inflict such terrible pain—almost more than Luca had been able to endure. He would see now how that one liked the same treatment. He would give the man time to hear about his friends, and consider... Luca could wait. It is worry that puts wear and tear on a man's head, often bringing about errors in judgment and the inevitable poor decisions. *Yes, it would be better to wait a bit and let the knifeman suffer.*

It was fully three days before Luca ferreted out the final assailant. By then the man was fully aware of the fate of his three *compañeros* and through local talk, knew who was responsible. He then took extraordinary steps to protect himself, going so far as to remove himself entirely from his usual haunts. He went to stay once again with his old father on the little *ranchito*—the impoverished surroundings which had caused him to leave for the bright lights of Guaymas, and his ill-considered new life.

For three days the man stayed in his father's squalid little house, pacing the dirt floor during the day, and at night tossing and turning on the same ratty bed he had once slept on growing up. His father drank *mescal*, and for the most part was either drunk... or crazy from being drunk. He offered no advice and spent much of his time sleeping.

The son, unable to sleep, started at every noise and leapt to the front window at each new sound. He dared going to the outhouse only in the dead of night and held out as long as he could each time, then went through the elaborate ritual of peering through each window, searching every inch of the yard, the broken corrals, and chicken coops he knew so well. He looked for the slightest thing out of place—hoping that would prove warning enough.

He had a gun, of course, two in fact, his own automatic pistol, and his old father's long barreled shotgun that he himself had used as a boy. During the day he was never out of reach of either—carried the pistol in his waistband, and at night hid it under his filthy pillow and propped the shotgun near at hand. He had never known such fear, even when conscripted into the military for his obligatory two-year stint of service in the Mexican army. Posted to the rampant violence of Ciudad Juarez, he had nearly lost his life on several occasions and thought he had become hardened in the process. He saw now this probably was not the case.

He woke his sleeping father and half-dragged him to the window to stand watch with the single-barrel shotgun, then opened the creaking old door and made his desperate run for the refuge of the privy—pistol gripped tight in his right hand—feeling safe only when he slipped inside and slid the wooden bolt into place. He was still holding the pistol in the air as he was struck a blinding blow to the side of the head, not enough to cause full loss of consciousness, but hard enough to rattle his senses and cause the gun to fly from his hand and into the evil morass of the toilet. Retrieving the weapon was unthinkable, but still he dove for the hole with every intention of making the effort, and immediately felt his head pushed into the vile opening and held in that choking, caustic, atmosphere, causing him to gag, unable to catch his breath or throw off the weight of his attacker.

"You see how it is, my friend?" Luca's voice was calm, almost sympathetic. "It hurts a little now, does it not? …But not as much as it will later, I can assure you." There was the sharp and unmistakable sound of a switchblade springing open, and Luca began the more delicate work that only so narrow a blade can do with any sort of precision. The knife had been honed to a razor edge and with each stroke of the sharpening stone the exact blueprint of its future work had been planned. Luca had an exacting knowledge of butchering pigs, and man is so like them that it was no trouble slipping the blade between the ribs and into the one kidney… no more than that… He didn't twist the blade before sliding it back out. He wanted this to last a while. The man screamed into the black hole, but Luca thought he would barely be heard outside the little privy. Since his own beating, Luca's hearing had not been the same, and he was not so sure what anyone listening might hear, nor did he care. He took his time now, probing, incising, but never so much as to cause the man to faint or give up the hope of life entirely… just enough to prolong the excruciating agony. By the time Luca had cut several tendons including those of the wrists and the big ones inside the elbows, the man had come to the realization that even should he survive, life would no longer be worth living. He now prayed to die, but that was not part of Luca's plan. He would cut the man's Achilles tendons as well, and then let him go. The hope was to someday see the pitiful wreck of this person going about Guaymas on padded knees and elbows begging for the *pesetas* to feed himself... not that he would actually be able to feed himself of course. He would have to eat from the ground like a dog. Now that would make a suitable and lasting atonement.

The old man in the house had been running from one window to the next, wondering what could be taking so long at the privy. Several times he thought he heard noises from the little building and once imagined he saw the door of the shack tremble. Twice he had called out for his son but heard nothing in return. He did not think it wise to go and see for himself what the matter might be.

When, at last, Luca thought there was little fire left in the man, he moved to begin the work on his heels. It was then the wretched creature reared up and hurled himself backwards against the beleaguered door, spilling them both out into the dirt and blackness. Luca was well aware there was someone watching from the house and intuitively rolled to one side.

Even as the blast and belch of flame left the window, the old man realized his mistake, but by the time he had opened the gun and inserted another shell, the intruder had disappeared into the night, leaving the father to contemplate the ruined state of his son... He did not yet realize what a great favor he had done him.

In the darkness Luca gnashed his teeth and cursed that death should cheat him of his full vengeance. After a while, though, he took it as a sign, and was not so disappointed. Word of what he had done would get around, and that alone was some consolation. People would know then what it meant to deal unfairly with Luca Tarango.

~~~~~~~

By mid-afternoon and far below, Luca spotted a lone follower and smiled. The tracker was headed in a direction that would take him well below this newfound refuge. It was one of the three *Indios* all right, and it was plain from his stride that he was tiring. Luca smiled at the frequent rests the man took, rests Luca himself would not have needed. *Good! Maybe the other two had finally become weary and turned back, leaving only this cabron to be dealt with.* These people up here were not the caliber of the tough *Yaqui* trackers of *Mexicó.* He would watch, see where the man wound up and then perhaps, after dark he would ease down there and see what could be done about him.

~~~~~~~~

By sundown, Harley Ponyboy was having difficulty following even Thomas's sharp, boot-heel tracks. The ground was rocky and the fading light was playing tricks on his eyes. While the deep shadows made him and Charlie nearly invisible from above, he was not sure how much longer he could trust the sign. When finally he stopped to study the trail more closely, Charlie caught up to him, and that exact question was in *his* eyes when he whispered, "Do you think we should drop back down in the brush and wait for morning?"

"No." Harley had already considered this. "Thomas has been following this game trail for a good bit now. It's headed for that split in the bluff and might even work its way out on top eventually. Thomas knows that; he's trying ta get above that *ch* *olló.*" He pulled at one ear and then scratched his head. "The problem is, it's still a long way ta the top. He's not going to make it tonight, and maybe we can still catch up, if we keep after it... and don' fall off the mountain."

It was that last part that was beginning to worry Charlie; he had twice already slipped in the loose shale and nearly gone down.

In the fading light, Harley pointed out a considerable ledge bordered by oak brush and stunted cedar. "That little bench up there seems a likely spot for Thomas ta spend the night. The deer have got this trail beat out pretty good, and we should be able to follow it that far if there's any kind of moon at all." Harley and Thomas went back a long way and had always had each other's back. Thomas had rescued Harley from several runs of bad luck over the years and Harley was not one to forget.

While Charlie was not convinced, he fell in behind the stubborn little man, and feeling his way along in the gathering gloom, could only hope for the best.

# 11

## *The Cat*

By the time Thomas Begay reached the comparative safety of the ledge, he had already decided it was as far as he could make it that day and stood breathless, looking into the shadowy abyss below. Nothing moved that he could see, and he hoped his two friends had the sense to stay below rather than follow him up the steep incline in the failing light. However, he knew Harley when he was on a mission and did not rule out the two of them stumbling in after dark. Thomas watched until finally it became too black to see even the trail he had come in on. He moved to the back of the ledge and put down his meager supply sack and pulled out his blanket and a can of something to eat. The remaining piece of bacon tempted him as well, but only a fool would make a fire now. He pulled Charlie's .38 from the shoulder holster and laid it on his blanket. It had become a growing irritation, chafing to the point of distraction. It never seemed to bother Charlie, but then Charlie never wore it enough to be a problem. When he finished eating from the can (he still was not sure what it was), he sat in total darkness and waited for the moon. It would be a while yet. There was enough breeze sweeping up the mountain to rustle the scrub oak and mask the many little night sounds, and he inclined his head slightly that he might better hear. Still there was nothing.

He had nearly dozed off when a chill took him and he reached for his blanket and thought *I should pick up the gun before it gets in the dirt,* he thought: *Charlie wouldn't like that.* Drowsily, he felt for the gun and cursed the darkness, "Sonofabitch," he said under his breath and groped for the revolver.

A calm voice whispered, almost next to him, "I got it already, *esse.*" There was an unseen grin behind the words... then everything went completely black—not the black that comes from loss of light, but rather the dark and all-consuming vacuum that swallows consciousness.

When at last Thomas arrived at some semblance of rational thought, his head throbbed, and there was a warm seep of blood running into his ear. He tried to move but found himself bound with thin strips of his own blanket, and he had been shoved nearly to the brink of that great nothingness below. The moon was on the rise—a slightly thicker slice than the previous night—along with a brilliant array of stars, and they cast just enough light that Thomas could make out the *mojado,* who rocked back on his heels and was no more than six feet away. There was a glimmer of teeth as he took bites from a can. He carefully took another small sausage from the point of the big knife and chewed reflectively before wiping the blade clean. He felt at his belt and replaced the folded knife in its sheath before asking, "You awake, *Indio?*"

Thomas shifted his weight to one shoulder, the better to see, but there was barely enough light, even for that short distance. What he could see, however, sent an icy chill up his spine. This was not so big a man as he had imagined, but even in that light the scarred face and sunken eyes showed a capacity for evil. Thomas remained silent, watching to determine whether or not this was indeed a man, or perhaps something else altogether. Thomas Begay had been in numerous jails and seen many desperate men—but none quite like this, he was certain.

"After two days push'n, push'n' to find me... and now you don't got nothin' to say to me, *pendejò?* The *mojado's* face cracked a fragment of a smile. "I been wait'n for you and you little friends, *hombre*. But I guess you *compadres* had to go home to momma, huh?" Then, with his tongue against his front teeth, he made those three little tsk, tsk, tsk, sounds that are the universal indicator of regret or sadness. "You should have gone with them, *hombre*. You could be safe and warm in *tu casa, ahorita. Pero no, señore*, you gots to be a big man an catch the bad guy, eh? Well, you see how that turned out for you then?" Luca paused to peer at Thomas through the darkness. "I don' feel sorry for you, *Esse*. You bring this all on you ownself, and now you just gonna' have to suffer for it. This is how it is when a man pokes his nose where it don' belong."

The nature of this… apparition… was discernable in his voice, and bile rose in Thomas's throat at the thought of being at the mercy of this… he still was not sure it was a man… *Humans don't come and go like a night wind, with no sign or warning. This was the stuff of witches, for sure,* and Thomas's mind recoiled at the thought of such wickedness in human form.

The *mojado* finished his meal and unconsciously reached for his shirt pocket and tobacco. "You don' got no *cigarillos, amigo*? I could use a smoke …It's a long time now I don' got no smokes." He chuckled deep in his throat, almost as though to himself. "Don' no one smoke in this country?" Then he cocked an eye at Thomas. "Why you want to catch me so bad, *hombre*? I'm not nothin' to you. Why you want to cause me all this trouble?" He held the .38 up in the light of the moon and looked at it. "This is a nice li'l pea-shooter you got here. What you hunt with it? *ratonci-tos*? Mouses?" He laughed, ended with a cough from deep in the belly, and spit bloody phlegm over the edge. Something inside had been hurting his chest since the wreck, and it wasn't getting any better. He wiped his mouth and went on, "Well, I don' mind telling you, my friend, it don' look good for you… it don' look good at all. Where you leave you *truck*e, *amigo*? You didn' ride those *caballos* all the way from town, I bet you." He slapped his knee in the darkness and grew pensive. "Naa, *hombre*, I think you got a *trucke* somewhere." His voice fell to a whisper. "…and I bet you, I can find out where."

Thomas heard him lay the revolver down and reach into his pocket. When the click of the switchblade reached him, he didn't at first recognize it. Then it came to him—he and Harley had once traded their truck jack and spare tire for a cheap bottle of whiskey and a switchblade knife. It was from a seller of curios outside Gallup. Harley knew the man, and that he sometimes sold a little whiskey on the side. They drank from the bottle and nearly wore out the switchblade snapping it open and shut the better part of the night. He recalled the sound of it now and knew without doubt, this was what it was.

Thomas Begay knew what was coming, and though he had, more than once, been cut in bar fights, the thought of it still left him queasy. The quick slashing of the amateur knife wielder was generally shallow and at first nearly painless. Even should the cut be more serious, one might eventually bleed out without any real pain. So it wasn't the pain so much that caused fear of the knife, and yet most men he'd known were more afraid of a knife than they were of a gun. It didn't make sense… but there it was. Thomas had already seen the work of this *mojado*, and it was not that of an amateur, nor had it been the work of a switchblade… and so he had hope that he was not to be killed just yet.

"I got some bacon in that sack." Thomas spoke with a concerted effort, head still pounding and vision blurred. "It's just you and me up here now." He was trying to focus and keep his voice calm, friendly even. "A little fire wouldn't hurt anything. Some bacon and coffee would be good." Thomas doubted the man would go for it, but he desperately wanted to warn Harley before they stumbled in unawares. They would know Thomas wouldn't have a fire with the *mojado* in the area. A fire would definitely send a message.

"A fire?" The *mojado* canted his head, appeared to be considering it, and his eyes went innocently looking about for something to burn, then he slapped his leg again and broke into a tittering little laugh. "Really, *hombre*? *Verdad*? You think I am that stupid?" He rose to his feet and said, almost in a whisper, "What we are going to do now, *amigo*, might burn a little, but it's not going to be a fire."

Thomas lurched to a sitting position, steeled himself for what was coming, then instantly fell back into blackness.

When Thomas again came to his senses, there *was* a fire and bacon and coffee cooking, and the grey face of dawn seeping down the face of the sandstone bluff. Charley was sitting directly across from him, and Harley was watching breakfast sputter in a pan.

He found himself propped against the back wall, wrapped in a blanket—his head bandaged with a handker-chief. He was woozy, had a hard time focusing, and peered cautiously around the camp, as though he might see the person from the night before.

Charlie fixed him with a stare and asked, "How you feeling now, big boy?"

Harley chimed in, "I hope you feel better than you look," and moved around the fire with the cup of coffee he and Charlie had been sharing. "Try a little of this Joe—it'll put hair on your chest."

Thomas's mouth was dirt dry and he was unable to answer until Harley held the cup to his lips, allowing him a good swallow. He finally managed a weak croak, "He was here last night."

"Yeah," Harley grinned, "we didn't figure you tied your own self up." He gave Thomas another sip of coffee. "We heard talk'n before we even got close, had an idea what was up. We was trying to ease up without spooking him... then Charlie here knocked a rock off the edge." He gave Charlie a frown. "We figured we better go ahead and rush the place before something worse happened." Harley paused and his face took on an incredulous expression. "He wasn't here. The guy was just gone. Disappeared!"

Charlie nodded his head through the smoke of the little fire. "He never made a sound that we heard, and couldn't have passed us on the trail either... not without us seeing or hearing him." He stirred the fire with a stick and peered into the greying dawn. "When it gets a little lighter, Harley's going to try to find how he got away. Right now," Charlie smiled, "he's thinking the guy just flew off this ledge like a bat."

Thomas looked around the shadowy little camp and said quietly, "I been thinking the same thing myself."

"Well, I think we'll find he went out to the end of this ledge and found a way up or down. He must have eyes like a cat." Charlie wasn't quite ready to believe they were dealing with anything other than a man.

The three ate silently and contemplated the events of the night before. Though still suffering from the blow to the head, Thomas did ample justice to his share of the breakfast Harley brought him. Thomas wasn't a shirker when it came to eating, regardless of circumstance.

"You think you will be able ta walk out of here this morning while me and Charlie go after this fella?" Harley wasn't so sure Thomas was up to going with them. "We'll have to travel fast to catch up with this guy now. It's not going to be easy."

Thomas smiled weakly in the rising dawn. "I guess I can go with you all right." He turned to Charlie. "Don't even think you're going to leave me behind. I owe this guy now, too." His expression hardened. "And you know I always pay what I owe."

Charlie nodded, equally grim. "Okay... but we're not going to stop and wait on you every little while."

Thomas shook his head. "That'll be the day, when *you* have to wait on *me*."

Charlie started to rise, winced, then reached behind him in the dirt and pulled out the .38 Smith & Wesson. "Well now," he grinned, "The prodigal gun has returned," and began wiping the dust off the revolver with his shirttail, blowing on the cylinder, and making sure it was still loaded. He had thought he would never see it again. "I'll give it a good wash when we hit some water."

Harley Ponyboy squinted at him. "I don' think this guy we're after is much on guns. I believe he's a puredee knife man." He then stopped and thought to himself, *he won't be a knife man for long if I get him in the sights of this army gun.* He patted the venerable Krag rifle beside him and recalled the old saw, "Never take a knife to a gunfight," and smiled broadly at the other two, but didn't let them in on the joke.

Harley gathered their meager belongings while Charlie helped Thomas to his feet and held his arm for a few steps, until he saw his friend could indeed walk, but not quite as well as either of them hoped.

Charlie was not kidding when he said, "Remember, if you can't hack it, we'll damned sure leave you behind, and send someone back to get you."

Thomas shrugged. "We'll see who leaves *who* behind, college boy." As his head cleared, the grogginess turned to resolve. Thomas meant to keep up, no matter the cost.

As the sun inched above the horizon, Harley checked the far end of the bench for sign. "He did'n get out this way," he said, "...'less he can fly," and threw a concerned look at Thomas. While the others gathered what little gear they had, Harley moved past them to the trail they had come in on the night before, then whistled, "Here it is. Hard as it is ta be-lieve—he came right toward us when he heard us coming, jumped up that little outcrop there, and let us pass right beneath him, then took the trail back down, I guess. Here's his tracks right on top of mine and Charlie's, and headed down. We might have been what saved Thomas getting hurt real bad."

Thomas, now at his side, looked askance at the tracks. "You sure?"

Harley snorted. "I'm sure, all right. The guy's like a cat!" Harley moved farther down the trail. "But he's not going back down," he called over his shoulder. "It looks like he's cutting straight across the base. If he makes it around the mountain, he'll hit that sheep camp the herder told us about."

Charlie and Thomas exchanged anxious looks.

"Why didn't he go over the top?" Charlie asked. "That looks to be shorter."

Thomas glanced up the fissure that led to the top. "Too dark last night to climb that trail, and he knew it. He's going around, all right. He's trying ta find a road out of here—he was asking me about a truck."

Charlie thought about this for half a second. "Those people over there don't have a truck—their brother told us they have to pack in their groceries from the trailhead by packhorse."

Assuming it *was* a man, Harley thought he couldn't be far ahead of them. "He would not have been able to travel very fast up here in the dark... no matter how good he is."

"There's no telling what this guy can do," Thomas said. "I never saw anything like it." He looked around the ledge through bleary eyes. "Old Man Paul T'Sosi told me a lot of stories about *Yeenaaldiooshii* and how they can change into other creatures and escape pursuers... change right into an owl or wolf." As an afterthought he said, "He's a Mexican, all right, but not like any we know. Like Samuel Shorthair says, he's probably from that bunch of *mojados* that wrecked on their way up from Gallup the other day. He seemed almost like an Indian, but different."

Charlie could see Harley taking this in and nodding agreement, but said nothing to the contrary; he knew these beliefs ran deep in his two friends, and they were not likely to listen to anything he had to say to the contrary.

At midmorning they came across a little spring, one whose source lay deep in the bowels of the mountain. There wasn't enough water in those hidden reservoirs to last long without replenishment from rain or snow, but they would often produce a little water until well into July.

Thomas flopped down in the grass near the pool and began filling his canteen. The others did the same but kept an eye on Thomas to gauge how he was holding up. They knew he was hurting and were surprised he had come this far, considering the pace Harley set. The ugly gash on the side of Thomas's head bothered Charlie. He knew they had nothing to put on the wound, but he examined it anyway and retied the bandage. "We should get something on this, or it's going to get infected."

Thomas looked disinterested, his face drawn and sallow—he was clearly starting to tire. Still, it was he who first struggled to his feet. "You know," he said carefully, looking at Charlie, "Annie Eagletree's place is not too far down the other side. I hope they are okay."

Charlie nodded. "I already thought about that, but they are nearly to the highway, and I'm sure they've already heard about all this and are prepared. This is right up Annie's ally, what with all those cop shows she watches, and Clyde's a pretty good hand with a gun. I'm sure he's all over this by now."

Thomas looked away and said, "Clyde is like someone else I know—he only *thinks* he's good with a gun." He looked up the mountain. "It don't matter how good he is anyway; he's no match for this guy."

Harley interjected, "Well, there are several camps between Annie's place and here. I don' think there's too much ta worry about. What bothers me is, we don' seem ta be catching up ta this guy… I think we might be losing ground."

Charlie Yazzie was not one to worry a thing to death when once he set his mind to it. "Were going as fast as we can, and that's all we can do. Keep in mind, there will be search parties coming in from Teec Nos Pos again this morning." He nodded to the north. "I doubt they'll catch him, but they may damn well slow him down some. Just having to stay out of their way should do that. Let's hope so anyway."

Harley brightened. "He may not travel at all today... Because of those searchers, he may just lay up in the brush somewhere."

Thomas Begay nodded but did not seem convinced. "We'll see..."

Several hours later they could, indeed, see the sign grow fresher, and Charlie knew he had been right. Though they had not yet seen anyone from the search effort, there had been several fly-overs by small craft, including a fish and wildlife agency Piper Cub, and an FBI-leased Cessna. Charlie worried about that one a little. Agent Mayfield had made it quite clear he would prefer they stay out of the case. *There's no law against searching for cattle though* he thought grimly, as he fell in behind the other two. He kept a watchful eye on Thomas, who at first seemed to have trouble keeping his balance on the steep talus slope. But as the morning wore on, Thomas grew stronger. Some hidden reserve seemed to kick in, which caused Harley to smile. He had seen evidence of Thomas's recuperative powers many times over the years.

It was still early morning when they came to the sheep camp and saw they were too late.

~~~~~~

Luca Tarango was disappointed in himself. First, he had misjudged the persistence of the Indians—thinking two had quit and given up the chase; that had been a mistake. Not hearing them coming had been another. And while his poor hearing could not be helped, his arrogance in discounting those others so quickly was something he would have to guard against in the future. It is always a dangerous thing to underestimate one's adversaries, and he silently vowed not to let it happen again. There was more to these *Norteñoes* than he had first thought. That one on the ledge had shown himself to be more resilient than expected. He couldn't help but wonder how he would have held up under the knife. Luca could see now that these people were not so different from himself, at least when it came to that inner toughness required in a bad situation. No, he would have to be very careful indeed when dealing with these people.

He had traveled most of the night—taking it slow. He doubted anyone could follow his sign until first light. He stayed to the shelter of the bluffs and took advantage of what little timber there was. He almost missed the sheep camp, hidden in a little swale. He had been lucky to come in downwind, the smoke from a dying fire alerted him. He knew there would be a dog or two but thought that he might be able to wait in the rocks near the camp until the herder was gone, then see what they might have that could be of use to him, without raising an alarm… These people might have guns, and would likely know how to use them.

This side of the mountain was not so rugged, and should he get his hands on a horse, he might well be able to work his way out to a road, and a chance at a vehicle—a way north to Colorado, and Tressa. Of course, a vehicle would require a driver (he had never acquired that skill), so there was that.

As he crouched there in the predawn, he could not help but think of Tressa and the good life they had led there in their little village, each day running into the next, the only worry being what they might have for dinner, or if the hens would lay an egg for breakfast. The thought of a fried egg and refried beans rolled in a fresh hot tortilla caused his mouth to water, making the pouches of freeze dried food pale in comparison. All in all, he knew their time in the village would not seem like much of a life to some people, but there was a certain satisfaction in the sameness and knowing what the days ahead might hold. The making of adobe bricks was not an occupation that required a lot of thinking. *Too much thinking was not good for a person. It only led to dissatisfaction, and ultimately to… change. No, it was better the devil you knew, than one you didn't.* This was how Luca thought as he sat waiting and watching as a young boy quibbled with his uncle about going with the sheep. Though he could not understand what was said, he could plainly see the older man was adamant as he gently pushed the boy toward the corrals, called up the dogs, and watched as they rallied the sheep.

Luca saw there was only one horse left in the corral and waited for the man to go back inside the tent. There was no sense in bothering himself with this man if there was no need. There was trouble enough already, and as he waited his mind again drifted back to Tressa.

If only she had not prodded him to move to the city, things might still be as they once were. He became a little irritated with Tressa then and wondered if he could somehow talk her into moving back to their little adobe and the life they had known since they were children. Not likely, he knew, but these were the things that occupied his mind as he shivered there in the cold dead calm of first light—gazing down on a sheep camp that might mark the end of him. Luca Tarango was a man not usually given to introspection and it's attendant regret, but in this instance he couldn't help but feel a bit nostalgic for the life he once had led.

# 12

## *The Loss*

The boy had been sent out with the band of sheep just at daylight, leaving only his uncle and one horse. The horse was lame, and the man, Harvey Bitsinnie, had stayed in camp to doctor it, telling his nephew he could bring the other horse back at noon, and then *he* would go to the sheep—a few of them needed doctoring as well. *Always something needed doctoring* Harvey Bitsinnie thought as he headed down to the corral with his little bag of medicines. The horse had somehow injured a right front foot when they packed in their supplies the day before, and already it was swollen and pus leaked down the side of the hoof. Harvey thought *there is maybe a stob or a thorn still in there.* He opened the corral and saw the stranger crouching behind the horse and cursed to himself, whispering the common Navajo epitaph *máii* (coyote) a word reserved for all that was despicable.

~~~~~~~

Charlie Yazzie had taken the lead when they came in view of the wall tent and cedar corrals that served as a summer spike camp for the Natanii sheep operation, and he was first to see Harvey Bitsinnie lying in the mud of the corral. Though dead, blood still pooled from knife wounds in the herder's chest and right forearm. The lame horse stood almost over him and did not move until Charlie pushed it aside. It was obvious the *mojado* had come for a horse and been surprised by the luckless herder. There must have been cursing later when the killer found the horse to be useless.

Harley pushed past Charlie and gazed down at the body. "This must be the uncle who runs this camp. Since the sheep and dogs are gone, the boy must be with them. He's probably safe for now."

Thomas Begay, who had moved up behind Charlie, shook his head before raising his eyes to the mountain. Searching. "No one's safe until this guy is caught. He's not going to leave witnesses, if he can help it."

Harley nodded agreement, glanced at Thomas, and speculated, "I expect you are the only one ta see this man's face and live ta tell about it."

"Only in the dark—I couldn't see much of him, but he don't know that. I imagine I'd be gone too if you boys hadn't come along." As Thomas said this, another shiver passed over him. He shrugged it off and said, "I think he might be putting a spell on me." He knew only Harley would really understand and frowned at the skeptical look on Charlie's face.

Charlie shook his head and looked down before saying, "Don't start thinking like that. You'll think yourself into an early grave," and headed toward the wall-tent.

Always there was this talk of witches, and spells, and beings from the underworld to deal with. Fewer and fewer people believed in them as time went on, but even among the most modern-thinking, there still was the lingering thought of magic and the power of those who understood it. Charlie Yazzie was not one to take these traditionalists' premonitions of evil too seriously, yet even *he* was becoming leery of this *mojado* and his never-ending bag of tricks.

When Harley Ponyboy caught up with him, he could see Charlie was in no mood to discuss what "powers" their quarry might have. So instead, he just said, "He's for sure looking for a horse now. I suspect he's headed for the highway and a ride out of here."

When the two reached the tent flap, they paused and turned to see Thomas Begay still standing in the corral, but backed well away from the dead man.

The tent was in disarray, with the newly arrived supplies pulled out of the panniers and scattered about. They could not tell if there had been a gun of any sort as part of the gear, but Harley Ponyboy knew every camp such as this would have some sort of firearm to ward off coyotes and bears. Possibly the boy had taken the gun with him on his herding rounds that morning. If not, they were now dealing with an armed adversary, and one considerably more dangerous than before.

Thomas Begay was still at the corral when the dead man's nephew came riding back up the hill to the camp. Thomas spotted him at a good distance and went to greet him with the sad news of his uncle, and to send him back down the mountain to fetch the authorities. When Thomas came back toward the tent, his friends had gathered a bit of food and were again ready to take up the chase.

"Did you find the 30-30?" Thomas called, even before reaching them. "The boy said there *was* a rifle, and two new boxes of ammunition brought in yesterday. I've sent him for help... and told him we were going after the killer."

Charlie Yazzie shook his head. "No, we didn't find any rifle, so that means the *cholló* has it. We didn't see but one new box of 30-30 shells. I guess he didn't feel like packing more, but even at that he's got plenty."

Harley stood in the doorway of the tent, holding tight to the old Krag rifle. He sighed and said, "We'll have the range on him, but not near the ammunition. We're gonna have ta pick our shots, should it come ta that."

Thomas Begay filled his canteen from the water bucket beside the tent door. "The boy says it gets a little dry on up the mountain. Said we should load up here."

Harley was already sorting through the horse tracks left from the herder's supply run of the day before. It wasn't hard, and he quickly picked up the *mojado's* footprints moving up the mountain. The man must know there would be searchers up ahead and that this latest killing could only bring more. He would have no choice but to lay up somewhere until dark, at least that's what Harley figured he would do.

It was just after noon when they topped the first big ridge past the sheep camp, looked across to the next rise, and saw the faint outline of a trail winding upwards through the pines and cedars, one that would surely continue across the top and then on down to the trailhead and the road out to the highway. Somewhere in between, the mojado was lying up in the brush, waiting for them.

Only a short distance later Harley stood perplexed, as he examined the rocky path in front of him. "I've lost him—I'm thinkin' now he didn't stay on this trail any further than that last switchback. He still means to stay above us." Harley said this last with a finality that belied the doubt in his mind. He really didn't know where the man had gone and was now even more convinced they had been dealing with something other than a man from the start.

Charlie, while disappointed at this news, was more concerned with the very real worry that the man now had a rifle and ammunition. "If he's above us, he'll be laying for us with that 30-30."

Thomas, after falling slightly behind, had again caught up, and after listening to the other two talk, didn't seem deterred by the thought of the rifle, and in fact appeared even more anxious to get on with it. "That gun won't be effective over 150 yards, and with him shooting downhill, it'll be hard to zero in on us the first round or so. I don't think he's an experienced shooter either. I'm betting he'll miss his first shot, and maybe Harley can get off a round at him before he can bracket us."

Charlie looked down at the ground. "Well, yes, assuming he misses his first shot... What if he doesn't miss?" Charlie thought the other two were thinking in pretty loose terms regarding the actual probabilities and odds involved. "Don't forget, he has more ammunition than us; he can afford to fling a little lead."

Harley squinted thoughtfully up the mountain. "This old Krag is good out to about 300 yards... maybe more. Both guns are open sights, so were even there, and we still have the reach on him... I'm a pretty good shot too."

Thomas wasn't swayed by Charlie's doubts either. "If he does hit one of us with his first shot, that leaves two of us to locate him and knock him down." He nonchalantly adjusted the bandage on his head and then lazily scratched his chin. "I once shot half a box of shells at a buck headed downhill, and that was with a 30-30. It's not easy hitting a moving downhill target, especially with that short-barreled saddle gun."

Harley looked at the other two and almost grinned. "Well, I guess we better keep moving then."

Even Charlie smiled at this, and as he turned back to the trail, warned caution. "Stay under cover, take it slow, and keep your eyes open. It would be nice if he *didn't* get that first shot." He knew Navajo are born gamblers and willing to take the short odds when they are in their element and feel lucky. These two *Diné* were no different.

During the entire day none of them had seen a single searcher on that part of the mountain, but they had noticed several dust boils down country, pickup trucks or jeeps, or possibly even four-wheelers. These were in addition to glimpses of spotter planes, and far to the north—barely visible—what may have been a helicopter. The authorities were working the country, no doubt, but as usual, they were seldom in the right place at the right time. The vast and rugged expanse of the reservation was not conducive to finding a man who didn't want to be found.

# 13

## *The Ingraciada*

Luca Tarango sat under a slight rock overhang along a very steep portion of the trail, hoping to stay high and maybe see his pursuers before they saw him. For the first time in days he was beginning to tire. It was the pressure. Those *Indios* were finally taking the measure of him, and he was finding it harder to stay out ahead of them. While he hated to admit it, even to himself, the simple truth was, he was no longer young. In the old days he could run like a *Tarahumara*, those indefatigable mountain runners of Mexico's great Copper Canyon, and with the endurance of his *Yaqui* forebears who, while small of stature, were as tough and hard to kill as snakes. He was afraid those days were over now. The pace was beginning to wear on him. Even with proper food and rest, he knew he could never be as he once was.

He brought the rifle to his shoulder and sighted through the buckhorn sights. This gun was a short little thing, and though he had never shot one like it, he knew instinctively that its heavy bullets would not carry far, not with any sort of killing power. He had seen these guns in western movies with Spanish subtitles. They were meant to be carried in a scabbard on a horse and would do best at close range. His tormentors would have picked up a long gun by now, too, he supposed and he prayed it would be no better than this one.

He reached in his pocket and pulled out the worn and dirty business envelope from Tressa's last letter and for the hundredth time examined the address of the restaurant where she worked. He thought of her constantly, even to the point of it interfering with his ability to reason, and that could be dangerous. There was no doubt he would have to seek shelter now, at least until nightfall, when it might be possible to slip by those searchers lower down and near the trailhead. He was surprised he had not yet spotted any ground volunteers as he had the day before. Obviously there must be fewer of them today. That's the way these manhunts usually went—everyone eager to take part, until they found how hard it actually was to hunt down a man in rough country. The search, for the most part, now seemed relegated to the air, though they must know the sound of the aircraft would be warning enough for a man on foot. He had never been in an airplane, so perhaps things appeared differently viewed from up there; he would have to consider that possibility.

"Ah, Tressa, what have you brought me to?" he wondered aloud, and could not help but think back to when they had first met in the little village where they were born. She had gone as far as she could in the one room *escuela* they had attended. A number of years ahead of her in school, he himself had learned little—to read only the easiest words and scribble out a few of them in a nearly illegible hand. Even that was eventually forgotten, as he followed his father in the adobe making business. There was a little arroyo at the back of the village that had the perfect mixture of clay and sand which, when one added the right amount of water and tromped in chopped straw or even horse manure, made the finest kind of adobe bricks. There was not so much call for those bricks right there in the village, as everyone made their own for what little repair work was needed. And there was little new building being done. He couldn't remember when the last new house had been laid.

Had it not been for the turbid waters of their little stream from the mountains, there would have been no village at all. The water was just enough for a few *milpas* of corn and beans, and then only when planted in the old way. The corn stalks supported the bean vines, and the two of them provided shade for some squash—chilies had to live at the edge of the field to catch the full sun. "That's where chilies get their heat," his father told him.

Once a month a truck came from a larger town and carried away the fruits of the brick-making trade and brought them the pittance that allowed them even so meager an existence. And so life went on, one day following the next, and with little hope for anything better. Eventually one forgets about hope and only concentrates on getting through the next day... *that* becomes the hope... that you will somehow get through the next day.

Tressa, though younger than he, and a haughty girl from childhood, claimed she was of Spanish blood, as poor girls from that region sometimes did, hoping to enhance their chances of finding a good husband or some other opportunity that depended on status and blood. Luca doubted there was a teacup full of Spanish blood in that entire part of the country. The only Spanish either of them had was their surnames, which no doubt were handed down from a church official in the distant past. No, Tressa was pretty much all *Indio,* just as he was, not quite as dark as some but *Indio* nonetheless. He never argued the point with her and allowed her to go on saying she was other than what she really was, a *mestizo* at best, and try as she might, she would never be more... not in that village.

They had, at first, expected children, and Luca still thought that might have made a difference. But it was not to be. Neither of them knew whose fault it was or how the situation might be remedied. There was no doctor beyond the very expensive ones in the city, and aside from lack of money, there was the usual chance they would be turned away for not being the class of people the doctor wanted seen in his office, though some of those offices were themselves nothing to be proud of. The couple had, of course, sought out the local "healers" in various villages—ones who would take produce, or chickens, or such in payment. Some of the treatments were quite complicated, entertaining even, but none produced the desired results, and in the end the couple had just given up.

Tressa said, "I'm through with these smelly, dirty, old people prodding and poking at me, shaking rattles in my face, and making me spit in my hand to read if there are children in my future. What does spitting have to do with having children… or rattles, or chants for that matter."

Once they had moved to the city and had money and learned to present themselves in a reasonable fashion, they had twice been examined by what they were told were creditable physicians, but nothing came of that either, and eventually they resigned themselves to a childless life, and still did not know what the problem was or whose fault it might be.

# 14

## *The Witch*

When finally darkness came, Luca still had seen neither hide nor hair of his three pursuers and could only surmise they had at last lost his trail. He *had* seen, far below and in the distance, one or two stragglers from the day's search parties. None of them had enough gumption to climb the mountain, preferring to do their looking where the looking was easiest. Eventually, he was able to rest and ate three meals in a row from the canned food taken from the sheep camp. The packets of freeze-dried food were now nearly gone, and while he would miss their light weight and variety of choice, it had been a good bit of trouble getting the preparation just right, for he seldom allowed himself the luxury of a fire.

There was a better moon this night, which along with the stars provided a surprising amount of light from a near cloudless sky. Even so, the darkness had caused him to end up on a trail that, while not in the exact direction he wanted, was so decent a path and so easy to navigate that he stayed with it, thinking he would find a better sense of where he was at first light. The easier pace lifted his spirits, to the point he was humming under his breath an old *ranchero* melody that had just popped into his head, one of those things that sticks in your brain, an "earworm" some called it, something that's only cure is to run its course.

The approaching dawn found him well down a narrow canyon, and he passed through pockets of warmer air from the red walls that still held a bit of heat from the day before.

As he came to a turn in the path, he saw below him a mud hut nestled in the crook of a tiny ribbon of water, no more than a trickle. He hunkered down and studied the dwelling. He had not seen one like it—more just a mound of earth covering a stone-and-stick frame, as far as he could tell. There was a black iron kettle suspended over a small fire, and to one side a coffee pot sat in the heat of the embers. There was no one around that he could see, not even a dog or sign of livestock. He would have thought the camp abandoned, if not for the fire and a small loom beneath a cedar tree. There was something half finished in the frame, but the light still was not enough to discern what that might be.

Luca took his time easing down the trail, pausing every little while to study the camp as ever more light played into the canyon. Whoever lived there was either inside or was away from the area entirely. He could see the camp quite clearly now, and there was no sign of any living thing. He approached as closely as the sparse cover would allow and crouched behind a little pinion tree, and watched through the branches... and listened. Only the faint crackle and pop of the fire disturbed the silence. The odor of fresh coffee floated on the tiniest of breezes, and his mouth watered at the thought of it. He leaned his rifle against the tree and had almost decided to move closer to the fire, when a woman's voice asked, "What do you want?"

He did not whirl about as most would have done. In his experience that might provoke instant aggression—for all he knew, she was holding an axe above his head. He remained motionless and took his time assessing the situation. It was a small voice, not particularly threatening, and showed absolutely no fear—there was no need for violence, not just yet.

"Coffee," he murmured.

The woman swept past him without another word, went to the fire, and without looking back, busied herself with the pot.

When she turned, they saw each other's face for the first time, and neither was impressed, nor concerned, with what they saw.

He rose slowly and moved to the fire. She was not at all like he had imagined from the voice—taller, older, plain looking, and absolutely nothing about her reminded him of Tressa.

The woman was watching him from the corner of her eye. "You are him... the one they are looking for down below." It was not a question.

There was no reason to deny it. "Yes." He reached across the fire, took the cup she offered, and sipped, almost daintily. "Where is you man... *tu familia?*" he asked and was curious beyond what the question implied.

She answered, nearly spitting the words, "I have no man... no people."

This information bothered him and he couldn't be sure why. "Not even a dog?"

"Not anymore... he's dead... snake bit."

He considered this, then squatted down on his heels and sighed from deep in his lungs. "You don' got no *caro...* no *trucke*? How you get to town?"

"I'm a witch," she said simply, as though it were common enough.

Luca raised his hands and waved the fingers in appreciation. "*Un Bruja?* You fly off to town on a broomstick?" He made a worried face. "How you carry you groceries home?" He chuckled, which caused him to cough. When he spit into the fire, there was blood on his lips, and he wiped his mouth on one sleeve.

The woman saw, but said nothing. She had seen tuberculosis many times on the reservation—but the man looked too healthy for that. There was something else wrong with him. One arm seemed barely usable, and there was evidence of other injuries as well—those things she might fix. But there was little she could do should it be tuberculosis. "You a Mexican?"

"*Si... un Mexicano.*" He looked her over. She wore a blue velveteen blouse and long skirt of the same material, but darker. "You an *Indio,* I guess, like me. What you call these *Indios* 'round here?"

"Navajo... but I'm some Piute too." She raised her eyebrows and pushed her chin to the north, from whence her mother had come and watched to see if being part Piute mattered to him as much as it mattered to others.

In those long ago times when the Navajo moved against the Piute from the south, and the Utes made forays from the north. They, between them, had torn her people apart. Life was cheap back then. The two more powerful tribes carried off women and children in plenty, and horses, trading them back and forth like silver *conchos* from a leather belt.

Now, in more modern times, the memory of it was still there, and feelings ran deep in certain clans. Her mother had been a healer in the north-country, but her brand of Piute medicine had not been so popular with these *Diné*... There was always that stigma in the back of their minds, and thus the chants and magic did not work so well for them.

"Me... I am *Indio,* too." He didn't put on airs, like Tressa. "*Yaqui*... maybe a little *Seri.*" He shook his head. "*Quin sabe.*"

She nudged her chin at the backpack. "Ah, just passing through... like a *tourista?*" she said then smiled, and whispered, "They say you kill people?"

He leaned forward so there would be no mistake. "Sometimes... when there is the need." And this was enough for the woman. In that moment she made up her mind about him and knew all she needed to know. She sat cross-legged on the ground, skirts swirled around her, elbows on knees, face cupped in her hands, and she smiled as she stared silently into the dying flames. The woman's dreams had, for a long time, foretold this coming—surely this was the person she had been waiting for.

~~~~~~~~

Harley Ponyboy was disgusted. The three of them had spent the entire morning searching for some sign or track of the *mojado,* and all without the slightest bit of luck. It was as though he had disappeared off the face of the planet or "flown away like a hoot-owl," as Harley put it.

He might be anywhere in Thomas's opinion. Charlie finally agreed—they couldn't just keep wandering around without a clue. Finding him without knowing the direction he had taken would be nearly impossible. He may already have gained a half-day on them, and still they could only guess where he was headed. Probably, they agreed, he would continue north as that had been his drift all along. The road was in that direction, and therefore the possibility of a truck. The man had mentioned wanting a truck to Thomas. But they found no sign of him to the north, either.

Finally, in a sweat, Harley threw up his hands and cursed several times, something he seldom did. "We are wasting our time here while that *chollo* is getting farther away. We may as well head down ta the road and see if we can't catch up with him down there. We know he'll wind up somewhere down there sooner or later." He looked over at Charlie and tilted his head toward Thomas Begay. "This guy ain't lookin' so good." He squinted his eyes at Thomas and shook his head. "He needs that cut fixed, and pretty damn quick too." The wound was obviously infected. Thomas himself, when forced to admit it, said he had a splitting headache, and the vision in one eye seemed dim. Back at the Natanni's sheep camp, Charlie had daubed the wound with a blue horse medicine from Harvey Bitsinnii's vet kit. It was what people commonly used on both humans and livestock, but in this case it had not seemed to help, and in fact, seemed to make things worse. Charlie had also found an out-of-date vial of penicillin, the shade-tree veterinarian's go-to cure all, but the contents seemed viscous, off color, and the rubber stopper showed signs of many needles. He decided against it.

By the time they were halfway down the mountain, Thomas began to shiver, and though he was sweating, he complained of the cold. The trailhead, when they came upon it, caught them by surprise, and relief was plain on their faces. Still, it was another good six or seven miles to the highway, and would be a long slog out, should no one happen by and offer them a ride. Thomas was beginning to stumble, his balance seemed off, and Harley was starting to wonder if they should just leave him beside the road and hurry on for help. When he glanced over at Charlie, he could see *he* was thinking the same thing.

As luck would have it, they had gone no more than a mile when an old green Ford pickup with a faded U.S. Forest Service logo on the door appeared, pulled over, and waited for them to catch up.

The driver was already standing beside the truck and peeing by the time they got there. "You boys look like you could use a ride," the boy said, zipping his pants. He had a wild shock of black hair that hadn't seen a comb in a while, and he seemed almost too young to be driving. "I only have room for two of you up here in the front," he said opening his door, "but one of you can jump in the back—be careful of that saw back there." There was a good pile of firewood in the bed of the truck, and a greasy orange chainsaw nested precariously in the middle of it.

Harley Ponyboy elected to ride in the back and shook his head as he wedged the saw into a bare spot next to the cab. *How much trouble could it be to put it where it belonged in the first place. Kids.*

Charley tried to help Thomas up into the truck, but he shook off the hand and boarded without support. He was hurting, dizzy, and in no mood for sympathy.

Charlie shrugged, climbed in beside him, and rolled the window halfway down. The cab smelled of gasoline, sawdust, and stale sweat. "We appreciate the lift. Seems there's not many people out today."

"No," the boy answered, "but there was a God's plenty of them yesterday. Most of 'em had to go back to work today, I guess."

Charlie looked at Thomas, whose eyes were already closed, and he was beginning to make little snoring noises. Charlie had to lean forward and talk around him when he asked, "Heard anything about how the search for that killer is going?"

"Well, I heard they haven't found him yet. That's as of this morning, when I left the house. That's about all you hear on the Navajo station. Those white boys in charge of the search couldn't find their ass with both hands. Most of the Indian volunteers quit the first day… said the authorities had them running all over the place… They claimed the group leaders had no idea what they were doing. And those fancy hound dogs they brought in were so confused by all the people, they couldn't pick up a trail." He laughed, reached down beside the seat, and came up with a bottle. "You fellas look like you could use a drink."

Charlie eyed the bottle and almost took the boy up on the offer, but glancing over at Thomas and then through the back window at Harley, said, "No, I guess not. These other boys don't drink, and I don't want to get them started… again."

The boy nodded wisely as he unscrewed the cap with his teeth and took a healthy swig. "I'm trying to quit myself."

Charley thought about pulling out his badge and lecturing the boy but was just too weary; besides, the kid had been good enough to stop for them. He'd maybe say something to him when they got where they were going. As the boy put the bottle away, he saw Harley in the rear view mirror, peering through the back window with a sad little look on his face.

Charlie studied the boy more closely and decided he was probably a little older than he first thought, but still not old enough to be drinking. "You lived around here long?" he asked him.

"Just about all my life, as far as I can remember." The boy wrinkled his nose and thought about it. "We never lived anywhere else, now that I think about it." He passed a hand over to Charlie. "I'm Lester... Lester Hoskinni."

Charlie shook hands and introduced himself, omitting the part about being with Legal Services. "I don't suppose many people actually live up this way?"

"Not hardly. The Natannii's sheep camp is up there in the summer, but other than that, there's only the old witch woman up Little Water Canyon. No one lives this high on the mountain year round."

Thomas bumped wide-awake at this mention of a witch. He'd only been dozing—he did that sometimes. He opened his good eye and fixed it on the boy. "What witch woman is that?"

The interruption caused Lester to lose his train of thought, but only for a moment. "Her name is Margaret, but everyone around here just calls her the witch woman. I don't believe I've ever heard her last name... if she's even got one." The road got a little better and he shifted up to take advantage of it. "She's only up here in the summers, gathers herbs and medicinal plants... stuff like that to take back home, over near Kaibito. Does a lively little trade in spells and potions over there, from what I hear. She's been coming here every summer since I was little. Says the plants on this mountain have special powers." He paused. "And there's magic crystals here, too—if you know where to find them. At least that's what my mother says the witch woman says. I was afraid of her when I was little... still am, I guess." He turned to Thomas. "I don't hold with witches, and neither does my family. They just don't want to mess with them...

you understand." He cut a glance over at Charlie. "Anyways, she's a Piute and you know how they are."

Thomas and Charlie exchanged squints. Charlie watched out the window, not really knowing what he was looking for, but knowing it was out there somewhere. He was nearly certain of that..

Thomas rubbed his bad eye and knew there would be no more sleeping for him. He turned to the boy. "Do you know Annie Eagletree and her husband Clyde? They live right out by the highway. Just built a new house across the New Mexico line. They run some stock on the other side of the mountain. We were looking for her cattle when our horses ran off."

The boy looked sideways at Thomas and ignored the question. "You fellas musta' got turned around some, huh?" There was a little something there in his voice, but it went away when he said, "Sure, we know Annie, and Clyde, too. Clyde bought my 4-H calf last fall. Outbid the Diné Bikeyah Cafe for him. Said he didn't want to see such a calf made into hamburger. Didn't mind paying for him either. Maybe you saw it when you were working their cows? He's a big boy, Hereford. Clyde said he was going to breed him this year." The boy was a talker for a Navajo kid; he sounded almost white, Charlie thought, and smiled when he remembered his grandmother saying the same thing about him when he was a boy.

"Do you folks have a phone at your place? I'd like to call over to Annie's and get one of them to come pick us up." Charlie nudged his friend in the ribs. "Thomas here needs a little medical attention. He fell off his horse a couple days ago, hit his head, and needs to have it looked at." Charlie usually preferred Thomas do all the lying, as he'd had more practice, but just this once and considering the circumstances, felt he was justified. Thomas nodded but said nothing—just made a frogmouth and stared out the windshield.

The boy had been wondering about the bandage on Thomas's head but had been too polite to ask in case it had been something embarrassing that caused the injury. Now he was glad he had waited—a Navajo doesn't just "fall" off his horse... *probably drunk,* was the boy's first thought.

When they pulled up to his parents' rust-streaked trailer-house, Lester again apologized for not being able to take them all the way to Annie's. "I don't have enough gas to get over there and back, and there's really no place to get any fuel this time a night. My dad usually keeps a five-gallon can in the shed, but I used it this morning to go get wood. They went to town for groceries this morning, so I expect he's already filling it in town." He grinned. "I doubt he wants me to miss a good day of wood hauling tomorrow."

It was Clyde that finally came for them. He recognized the Hoskinni boy immediately and shook hands several times during their conversation. He also remembered the calf he'd bought the previous fall and assured the boy it was now big enough to breed, was in fact out with the cows somewhere right now. Clyde frowned at Thomas and Harley when he said this, as he felt the two had been remiss in not bringing at least some of those cows back with them on their first little expedition. Regardless of circumstance, it had been their job to find those cows and bring them in, not run around the country scaring up dead people. Clyde did own up to a bit of responsibility. He knew he should have already had those calves branded... that, and that other little thing bull calves require to become steers—the very thought of it made him squeamish. He preferred not to think about it when he could help it. His wife, Annie, on the other hand, had no such reservations, and on branding day, usually brought back a bucket of "Rocky Mountain Oysters" to be filleted, breaded, and deep-fried. She declared them delicious and couldn't imagine anyone not liking them. Clyde had some funny notions, she thought, but excused him on the grounds he was raised in town and was the son of a schoolteacher.

Annie Eagletree had waited up, met them at the door, and then immediately bombarded her nephew with questions about the killings. She knew all about the search, and like everyone else was displeased with the results. "Right here on our own damned reservation," she said, and eyed Charlie as though it were his fault. Her many hours of watching television cop shows had left her with a good bit of information in regard to catching crooks, and she thought her nephew might do better should he listen to her advice now and then. She still regarded him as "the law," though he had many times tried to dissuade her of the notion.

Annie Eagletree was Charlie's grandmother's sister, but by clan she was his grandmother too, same as her sister, and while she knew he was not big on tradition, she was determined he not forget that part at least. Annie had no children and Charlie had always been her favorite. She had often sent him money and little packages of goodies when he was away at school—just so he wouldn't forget her. She now came close and put a hand on his shoulder. "When you find him, nephew, remember this about serial killers: they are always smarter than people think they are. Forget that, and he will kill you too." Charlie was a little taken aback but saw his aunt was deadly serious and filed the information away in his mind. He usually didn't pay much attention to his aunt's guidance, but this time he did, and gave her a peck on the cheek. Annie smiled, and was not at all embarrassed.

Charlie asked if he could borrow her phone, and she brought it to him on a twenty-five-foot cord. She was proud of this latest modern affectation and liked to keep it with her as she did her chores around the house. She thought it rude to make people wait past the second ring. Clyde was forever tripping over the cord and swore he would throw the whole thing out in the yard... but he knew better than to try it.

Sue answered on the first ring, and it took Charlie awhile to explain why he hadn't gotten in touch before now. And, why he hadn't been around the radio in his truck for several days either. After he told her how much he missed her, they talked about little Joseph Wiley and what he had been up to. She mentioned that Lucy Tallwoman had been by several times, wanting to know if Sue had heard anything. She hadn't heard from Anita as yet, but like Lucy, the woman didn't have a phone, and Sue thought it likely she had gotten used to Harley being gone. Sue's tone turned more serious when she told him Samuel Shorthair had called the house and left a message for Charlie to get in touch as soon as he got back—something about information he might like to know. Charlie told her that since it was so late, the three of them would spend the night at Annie's and go back up for his truck and trailer in the morning. Thomas, he said, was worried about the horses and thought they ought to locate them and get them back off the mountain. Sue didn't sound too happy about this but knew Charlie was only doing what he felt called to do. She told him she would call his office for him first thing in the morning, but then he said not to bother, as he would radio in when he was back at his truck. He didn't think the office would be open before then anyway.

Harley and Thomas stood close by, listening to the phone conversation. They grinned when Charlie told Sue he loved her. Even Aunt Annie wasn't used to that kind of talk in public and looked away so as not to embarrass him. When he hung up, Charlie turned to Thomas and asked if he wanted Aunt Annie to look at his head or just have Clyde take him in to the clinic.

Aunt Annie snorted, "Clinic? For what?" She was known to be as good a vet as there was in the county, and seemed offended that anyone might turn down her services.

Thomas quickly agreed. "She can take a shot at it if she wants to. I don't think I need the clinic."

Annie smiled when he said "shot" and took him into the kitchen, where she unwrapped the now filthy bandage and held his head to one side to catch the light. "Well now, that's a mess. Charlie, get me some water and one of those clean tea towels from the cupboard. Harley, look in the icebox and bring me that new bottle of Combiotic… and a syringe. The syringes are in that box on top—the big horse sized ones—he's going to need a pretty good jolt." Thomas frowned at this and looked at Charlie, who shook his head and shrugged. After cleaning the wound and plastering it with antibiotic cream, Annie re-bandaged it and snapped the little metal top off the injectable. When she started pulling a good dose of it into the syringe, Thomas stood up and started rolling up his sleeve. Annie shook her head and waved a finger in front of his nose. "Drop 'em," she told him. "If I pumped this much juice into your arm, you wouldn't be able to use it for a week. I need a bigger muscle, and you know where that is."

Again, Thomas looked to Charlie and started to protest, but thought better of it when he saw the look on Annie's face.

"You'll need another of these tomorrow too," she said, "So you better get used to it. Maybe it'll learn you to stay outta' trouble." She'd known Thomas since he was a boy and wasn't about to cut him any slack. Harley stood grinning in the corner and nodded encouragement to each of them in turn.

The next morning dawned cool and cloudy with the essence of wet mesquite pulled up by the frontal system out of Mexico. When Thomas and Charlie came in from the spare bedroom, Harley—who had slept on the couch—had breakfast well underway. Thomas stood rubbing his hip, and glowered at Harley Ponyboy when he laughed.

Clyde was out refueling Annie's truck from the pump on the fifty-gallon drum by the tool shed, and by the time he came back in, Thomas had taken his second injection, this time like a man, and was already wolfing down a huge breakfast. He obviously felt much better. Still, Annie warned, he really should have a third shot the next day, should he be back their way. The night spent in a real bed had been good for all of them, and the generous breakfast Annie made available had them feeling like new men.

Annie looked askance at their clothing. "You boys should let me wash those duds for you before you go. They look about due." Charlie agreed about the state of their clothes but said they hadn't time and gave his Aunt Annie a kiss on the cheek before gathering up the food she had prepared for them and heading out to the truck. He had borrowed two rifles from his aunt the night before… and a considerable amount of ammunition. That way all three of them could be armed. There might come a reckoning, he thought, and he wanted them to be ready for it.

# 15

## *The Spell*

Luca Tarango was not a man to give his trust lightly, but there was something about this "*bruja*," this witch-woman, that he connected with. Nearly every village in Mexico had its own version of a witch, and it was the rare person who had not taken advantage of their services, though few wanted it known. A considerable amount of people's lives was thus spent conjecturing: whether or not a spell had been put on them, or if not, should they have one put against someone else. The evidence of these goings-on could be as minor as a sick goat, or as serious as a death in the family, and virtually nothing *bad* happened without it being laid at the door of a witch. Luca's own father had once paid a bruja to conjure up a spell against a woman who refused to pay for the adobes used in the repair of her house. His father had been disappointed when several days passed and nothing untoward happened to the woman. Come to find out, the woman had not known about the spell, but when the information was passed along to her, she immediately fell ill and suffered for weeks, before having a spell of her own put against his father, who when informed about *it,* fell seriously ill himself. And so it went, back and forth, until it became a way of life for some people—a source of entertainment for the entire village—but one that might indeed have deadly consequences.

*These Navajo must be the same as his own people when it came to witches*, Luca thought… and he was right.

The woman brought him a tea of red willow bark—the inner bark—mixed with some secret herb he couldn't identify. In only a short while he felt better, but very, very tired. She told him he should sleep and showed him to the hut, where there was a bed consisting of sheepskins and blankets. He knew it would be pointless, dangerous even, to continue his journey until the searchers quit coming in such droves. He decided this was as good a place to hide as any, at least, for the time being. As he drifted off to sleep, he seemed to remember the witch whispering something, but he couldn't quite make out what it was. Tressa now seemed very far away.

The witch had gone to the top of the canyon and there in the cedars built a little fire, no more than a few dry twigs, invisible, should one be more than a few feet from it. From her medicine pouch she took a pinch of purple sage and placed it atop the little blaze, where it smoldered a bit before releasing a tiny plume of smoke—no larger than a pencil it was—which lasted only a half-minute or so. But it was enough to wash her face in, and she wafted the smoke over herself with both hands in a cleansing ritual as old as time itself. Thus she cleared her mind of all but her immediate objective. At last those people who had pushed her mother from her own land, her own home, would pay the price for their cruel and haughty treatment. That those interlopers were of her father's people made no difference. And neither did her father's being one of them matter... No, he most of all would feel the heavy hand of her redemption.

When they first came to the upper San Juan and pretended to be friends to the Piute, the Navajo family settled themselves on a poor section of ground along the barrens of the river, all rock and sand, but even then her grandfather had warned that these *Dineè*, as he called them, were renegades and not to be trusted. Why would they come from the rich lands they claimed were their old home to settle in this desolate area of poor grass and little water, a land where even the Piute, who were born to hard times, had a miserable time of it. They must be on the run from someone or something in their own country, her grandfather said. Only a few good places, right on the river, had enough water to grow anything and the Piutes had held these plots since time beyond memory. Some had filtered in from the Great Basin, well before the Navajo. Now the Navajo wanted it, and while it took place before Margaret was born, the effect of it changed her life forever.

It did not take the newcomers long to move nearer and nearer to Margaret's family, until finally they were on the very boundary of the property and could be seen doing their morning business. There were two older boys in the group and several older men as well. The old grandmother and mother were seldom seen, kept to themselves, and did not come to visit, as was proper for ladies to do.

Though he was already an old man, Margaret's grandfather, as head of the clan, took it upon himself to ride to the trading post and inform the trader of what was happening. The trader, he told the family, would intercede for them with the authorities. It was only a few weeks later that her grandfather disappeared, never to be seen again. After that the renegade Navajos did pretty much as they pleased, and Margaret's mother and her mother's sister were forced through intimidation to "marry" the Navajo boys. Once the girls were pregnant, the outliers claimed they were now family, and when the government man finally made his way to those far reaches to investigate, he was assured by the head man of the Navajos that everything was fine and that they were all one big family now. It was not long after Margaret was born that her mother saddled a horse in the dead of night and, strapping her new daughter in a cradleboard, left that place for good. It was now only a lonesome country filled with bad memories.

Later, down in the towns, Margaret's mother remarried, but the new husband was little better than the first and was known to abuse her and her daughter "frightfully," in the words of the trader at Kiabito. When Margaret was only eighteen, her mother and stepfather both died when the man, drunk at the time, drove their car off a high embankment and into the San Juan River. She left Margaret a *hogan*, a few sheep and goats, and knowledge of medicine taught her by her Piute mother. Soon after, she was blamed for the first time of witchcraft, ostracized by the entire community, and after a while came to believe it herself. Slowly then, she built a reputation for powers beyond those of most healers. She learned how to use people's superstitions against them. She also learned an inherent distrust of men in general and never married. Most men who might have made suitable husbands listened to the talk and were afraid of her. One day, she knew, just the right person would come along—a merciless person who was not afraid, one strong enough to lay waste to those people on the upper San Juan.

Luca woke from his sleep and went to the blanket that served as a door and looked out. He saw it was almost sundown and the woman was at the fire preparing food and quietly singing some repetitious song, or chant. He felt better than he had in many days and knew it was mostly because of this woman and her medicine. When she looked up, she did not smile but indicated a place by the fire, and he went there and sat down on a section of log that had been dragged there while he slept. It had a folded sheepskin on it, and he could see the woman had gone to some trouble to fix it. The pot held a sort of stew, and while it was made of nothing he recognized, it had a pleasant smell to it and bubbled nicely in the pot. There were also tortillas warming on a flat stone, and he wondered once again how the woman got her supplies. He suspected it must be a long way to town, and that meant someone was bringing them to her.

He felt no particular gratitude toward this woman for the things she had done, as he knew they had been done for a reason, and eventually he would come to know what was required of him, and what he should do about it. He was a man who always paid his debts, be they for good or evil, and he would repay this one too, assuming the cost was not too dear.

"How did you sleep?" she asked, knowing full well that he had slept like the potion decreed he should sleep, but wanting to hear him say it. That was important.

"I sleep all right... I don' dream so many bad things, like sometimes."

She poured a cup of coffee from the pot and brought it around to him. "There is no cream or sugar – *no leche, o asucar,*" ...She used up a good portion of her small supply of Spanish to make sure he understood.

He nodded. He seldom took milk or sugar in his coffee but did not say this, as he wanted her to think the lack of these things *was* an inconvenience, and thus figured less gratitude would be required on his part. He considered it best to play the game as she contrived it, and give nothing away.

In olden times when an Indian gave a gift it was with the expectation that one would be given in return, hopefully a better one. And while the giver might then protest, in the end they would take the return present and be satisfied. Should one not have a better gift to give, he might just mention that he had the person in mind for a certain thing and that it would be worth waiting for. Things were not so different even now, and Luca reached over to where his pack leaned against the end of the log, pulled it to him, and emptied his food on the dry grass, pushing it toward her, canned goods mostly, from the sheep camp, and with the odd packet or two of left over freeze-dried in the mix. It was not so hard to get food in this country that a man could not pay what he owed. Thus the man and woman revealed themselves, one to the other, but only bit-by-bit.

The woman filled his bowl from the pot, put a spoon in it, and passed it across with only a glance at the things he'd offered. But she was pleased, nonetheless, and showed it as she caught his eye and smiled. Things were going quite well in her opinion.

"How you get you food out here?" This was the second time he had asked the question, and now wanted to hear her answer. Though it was pretty obvious someone was bringing her things, it would be good to know how and when this happened. If he were to be there a while, it might save them both some unpleasantness.

She tilted her head to one side and looked long and hard at him before answering. "The trader sends an old man, his helper, every two weeks. Sometimes he don't come when he's supposed to, but mostly he does... when his truck don't break down."

He nodded at this, as though satisfied with the information—he tucked away the part about the truck. The stew was good, whatever it was, but he politely refused another helping, saying he was not used to eating large amounts and was full. The woman disappeared inside the *hogan,* and when she came back, she brought a hard black twist of traditional tobacco. He had not thought it available in this country, though it still could be had in Mexico if you knew where to find it. The woman used the tobacco in various little ceremonies, she said, just as people had for many thousands of years.

He could not help but show his pleasure as she handed him the tobacco and a small packet of papers. He crumbled a bit from the end of the twist into a little line on a paper and rolled it, licking the edge. When he took a burning twig from the fire and lit the end, smoke rolled from the corners of his mouth, and he laughed outright and was happy. He sat back and inhaled and a great contentment fell over him as he sat at his place by the fire, in a land so distant, his uncles would wonder at the daring of it all. He had only a few dollars left of the money those uncles provided him at the start of his journey, and he pulled this out and placed it on the little pile of canned goods. It occurred to him that he should have taken the money from the dead *mojados* in the wrecked van that night, but it would not have been very much, probably, and what little they had would have been sewn into their clothing; there had not been time for that. Even the *coyotero* had left the bulk of the money he'd collected in the hands of his brother, before leaving Mexico. He'd made it obvious, too, that he handed over that money—one could not be too careful in this business. There were always one or two chancy characters in every bunch.

In any case, Luca Tarango did not steal from the dead. That was not his line of work.

While he was thinking these things the Witch Woman came close and plucked at his shirt, saying she had something to tell him and whispered in his ear that she knew a very powerful charm... something no one else had knowledge of.

"What is that?" Luca asked innocently.

He could barely make out the words as she mouthed them. "I can make you *invisible*," she said, and looked this way and that before going on. "I have a crystal I found only this spring. It is what brought me the dreams that foretold your coming." She looked to the heavens, where the stars were beginning to show, and seemed for a moment to be lost in the discovery of them. She spoke again, but only when she was satisfied he understood the enormity of the thing and could fully grasp its implications. "With the magic of this crystal and the spell I will teach you, no one will be able to see you, even in full daylight. You will, at last, be able to do what is in you to do... and no one will know." She brought forth a small violet-hued crystal and held it to the heavens, stared through it at the stars, smiled, and then began speaking in a tongue he didn't know. With wild supplication she called upon whatever deities she served, and when she finished, she passed him the crystal and spoke in a near normal voice, "An old Piute woman taught me this charm—it will only work once, so you must use it only in case of desperate need."

This was nearly beyond his comprehension, and his eyes grew wide at the very thought of such witchery. She spent a long time repeating the few words of the incantation and made sure he could say them just so, and in exact order. She showed him how to hold the crystal in the proper way and press it tight against his breast. When finally she thought he had it, he watched as she backed away from the fire to go alone to that secret place where she prayed and did—he knew not what. He put the crystal in his pocket and thought he felt a certain heat from it, and that feeling returned each time the crystal came into his thoughts. And while the woman still did not have what she needed from him, he now had all he needed from her, and he thought about this long and hard before making his final decision. It was Tressa that played on his mind.

The woman had not taken any of the money or food he had laid out for her that night... but the next morning they were gone just the same.

# 16

*Treachery*

Clyde dropped the three of them off at Charlie's truck as the sun broke just above the edge of the sage flats. A mist lay across the grey-green scrub until the first rays caused it to disappear. The old woman, She Has Horses, was gone when the two went to see about her, and there was only a sad emptiness in the vacant eyes of the *hogan* and open-gated corrals.

Thomas and Harley started for the hidden canyon where Thomas had turned loose the horses. But they would first see if the people at the sheep camp knew where those horses might now be. When last Thomas had talked with the herder, the young man said he would try to locate the animals and put them in with their own stock until someone came for them. Harley carried the old Krag rifle with the intention of returning it to his distant clan relatives and hoped, with their help, to gather the saddles they'd left behind. They were to meet Clyde that afternoon down country—the thought was to later rendezvous with Charlie if possible.

Thomas had remembered to borrow cinches and other tack to replace that which the *mojado* had destroyed, as they would still have to ride the horses out to the trailhead. Harley thought they could cut many hours off their previous trip by going cross-country. He worried at how far the *mojado* might be getting ahead of them and what mischief he might be up to.

Clyde was supposed to be waiting for them with a stock trailer at the lower trailhead that afternoon. In the meantime Charlie would get Samuel Shorthair on the radio and see what the tribal policeman might have learned, though he rightly figured Sam would not want to disclose any critical information over the radio. Charlie would, in the end, probably have to run by the command post set up for the searchers, and he would have to do it early, if he wanted to catch Sam Shorthair before he left. It would be a long day for all of them, and Charley asked Thomas again if he was up to it.

"I'm up to it, all right." Thomas grinned. He knew Charlie needed to stay with the radio for at least a while yet that morning, and then too, Harley would need help with the horses.

Lester Hoskinni had told them the authorities gathered their forces each morning not far from the Hoskinni camp. Charlie figured Sam Shorthair was already en route and FBI Agent Mayfield probably was as well. That might prove a bit sticky.

When Charlie was finally able to get through to Sam, he could barely make him out, even though he was not that far away. "Sam, you're breaking up..." The red sandstone ridges that separated them were hard on radio waves. Some said it was the iron oxide that blocked the signal; still others thought it some sort of magnetism inherent in the formation. Maybe it was both. He only knew he was out of luck this morning. His radio sputtered and popped and sounded like bacon frying in a pan, and after trying for nearly ten minutes to decipher odds and ends of conversation, Charlie reached down and silenced the unit with a twist of the squelch knob––his ears needed a rest. Near as he could tell, Sam had said he would be there in about an hour, but he could have meant something else entirely. He wondered if Sam Shorthair knew about the "witch woman" up Little Water Canyon.

As he approached Lester Hoskinni's place, he saw him out in the yard with an older man. They appeared to be unloading firewood from the day before. On impulse, Charlie pulled into the yard and beeped the horn, which set off the dogs, and Lester turned to threaten them with a stick before walking over to Charlie's truck. The older man, who looked a lot like Lester, must be his father, Charlie thought. The man stood looking across at them with a frown. He wanted his truck unloaded and for Lester to be on his way back up the mountain. He liked to keep a good supply of wood on hand—if the roads got muddy, they might not be able to get back up there for a while. They were calling for rain on KTNN, "Voice of the Navajo Nation". The old man was a believer and took no chances.

Lester was grinning as he looked at the tribal insignia on the truck. "You didn't say you were the law." Anyone with an official truck was "the law" to Lester.

"I'm not." Charlie smiled back. "If I were, I would have arrested you yesterday for drinking."

Lester, still grinning, turned to see if his father had heard, but saw no sign of it. "He'd kick my ass if he knew I had a bottle."

"And he should too," Charlie said, and didn't smile when he said it. "Anybody been up the road this morning?" he asked as he looked up the highway toward the access road.

"No, not that I've seen, and I'd of seen them if they had." He paused and reset his baseball cap, which was turned around with the bill in the back. He pushed his chin toward the highway. "Several tribal trucks went by earlier, and one of them stopped by. Tribal policeman asked had we seen anything suspicious." He reset his cap again. "Hell, my dad thinks everything's suspicious, but he don't talk much to cops, so I told the cop everything was about like it always was." He chuckled. "He told my dad, in Navajo, 'to be on our guard, and be on the lookout for strangers,' like we don't have a radio, and don't know what's going on. I doubt any-one would get by our dogs anyhow."

Charlie looked at the dogs, big mixed breeds both of them, and nodded thoughtfully. "Maybe you better take one of them with you this morning."

Lester's father was motioning for the boy, and Charlie waved a hand his way. "Looks like you better get back to work. The cop was right. Be careful up there today. Nobody knows where that guy will show up next." He hesitated as he turned toward his truck. "...And lay off that bottle! You might not be so lucky next time you give someone a ride."

The search party was gathering at the state highway department's temporary maintenance pull off, and Charlie spotted the tops of the gravel piles before the parking area came into view. Even though Lester had mentioned it, he was surprised to see how few civilian and private vehicles there were, not over a half-dozen, he thought. There were four or five nondescript hounds tied to a truck bumper and an old white man trying to untangle their leads. The dogs didn't look all that interested in going out either. He spotted Sam Shorthair's pickup and angled over toward it.

Sam rolled down the window and had a worried look on his face as he hung up his radio mic. "I heard you on the air earlier," he said, "but couldn't understand more than a few words. We're working off the old relay transmitter up here, and the coverage is spotty at best."

"Same here. I suspect it might be better up higher, but down there in the canyon we may as well not have radios."

Sam indicated a black Suburban on the far side of the parking area, partially obscured by the gravel piles. "That's FBI over there. There's three of them now. Agent Mayfield must have called in the cavalry last night. I guess you heard I'm the new liaison officer between tribal police and the Feds. I've already had a little chat with them this morning... and it didn't go well either."

"Congratulations, Sam," Charlie said, ignoring the last part. Privately, he thought, *I don't envy you your position.*

*Agent Mayfield isn't someone I'd want to spend much time with.*

Sam nodded his thanks. "Well, I sort of had it thrust upon me, and I already may be off to a bad start. Mayfield insists we send everyone high this morning—said we weren't covering the upper area like we should. I almost expected him to say 'You lazy bastards...' but he didn't." Sam grinned. "He's from New York City, for God's sake. The only backcountry he's seen is maybe Central Park."

Charlie smiled at this. "Sue said you called. I'd have gotten ahold of you last night if it hadn't been so late."

Sam nodded again. "Where's your cohorts?"

"Off looking for lost horses. Clyde will pick them up down-country this afternoon, and they're supposed to meet me back here later today—depends on how quick they come up with the horses, I guess."

Sam took off his sunglasses and pinched the bridge of his nose, then carefully placed the glasses on the dash. "What I wanted to talk to you about is this guy we're after— looks like he probably *is* from that van that rolled over last week down on 491. FBI sent the vehicle identification to Mexican Federal Police, and when next of kin was contacted, the *coyotero's* brother told them there may have been a recent prison escapee named Luca Tarango in his brother's consignment of wets. A real bad boy from what the *Federales* told our people. Mexican federal authorities believe he's killed several down there. The *coyotero's* brother said no one knew *who* this "Tarango" person was until after it was too late to do anything about it. The guy fits with these killings up here, I guess." He looked over at the FBI car. "None of this information has been released as yet, and may never be. I'd appreciate it if you just keep it under your hat for the time being. The bureau did send off a crap-load of fingerprints from the dead illegals, but still haven't heard back on 'em... said they probably wouldn't hear either. I guess the system in Mexico is just pitiful when it comes to any kind of forensics."

Sam raised his eyes. "Mayfield says their main investigative technique is *beating* information out of people."

The tribal officer sighed and rubbed his temples with the fingers of both hands. "From our angle, I really don't know where to go from here."

Charlie thought he should be straight with Sam, and keeping one eye on the FBI car, lowered his voice. "There's a woman locals think is a witch. Her camp's almost to the upper end of Little Water Canyon. My topo map shows it to be right in the path of anyone who might want to avoid the main trails on their way down to the highway. I think you and I should at least check on her—let her know what's going on." He indicated the government car with his chin. "Agent Mayfield doesn't know this country, or the people, not like we do. It's our reservation, and I think it's up to us to bring this guy in." He stared directly at Sam when he said this, much as a white person might do, and though Sam was not a traditionalist himself, the gaze made him uncomfortable, and he was first to look away.

Sam knew he would be taking a big risk by throwing in with Charlie at this point, especially in view of the FBI's warning for Charlie to butt out. But, when Sam thought about it, he couldn't help but feel Charlie was right; it was their people, and this was their job.

When Sam and Charlie pulled out in Sam's truck, they had to drive right by the government car and saw Agent Mayfield start to roll down his window. They didn't stop or even look that way. Sam didn't want to lie about where they were going, or why. Eldon Mayfield was probably a decent enough guy in Sam's view, but he told Charlie it might take a little time for the government man to get used to how things were done on the reservation.

For Sam Shorthair's sake, Charlie hoped that was true.

# 17

## *The Twist*

It was still early when Margaret told Luca he should go off in the brush. Just like that, she told him, and she didn't look away when she said it either. "The old man will be bringing the supplies from town today," she explained, "and we don't want him to see anything that might arouse suspicion. I've known him a long time," she said, "but evil has a way of worming its way out of a person when you least expect it. I don't like surprises." She cautioned Luca not to come back or make any sound until he was sure the old man's truck was gone. The two of them brushed out Luca's tracks with juniper branches, and after he left, she walked back and forth and scuffed dirt so it would show only her tracks and wouldn't appear freshly swept.

Luca wasn't used to taking orders from women. Even Tressa had known better than that. But he said nothing and gathered up his water bottle and rifle, disappearing up into the rough ledges behind camp. On his own, he might have handled the situation of this deliveryman differently, and more permanently, but this wasn't Mexico. Maybe he should rethink how he approached things in this country.

Once above camp, he situated himself in such a way that he could look down on the crude dwelling and even a portion of the rutted track coming up the canyon. He thought he might have a long time to wait and fell into that secret zone that allows one to think of other things yet remain aware of the business at hand. The thought occurred to him that this witch woman might have played up to him only until she could safely get word to the authorities. But no, that wouldn't make sense; she could just as easily have killed him while he slept, or put something in his food, or any number of other things should she have wanted to rid herself of him. No, this woman had something else in mind. She was not so bad looking that she could not have found another man, should she have wanted one in that way, but he doubted now that she had any such interest in him.

Several times he had thought her on the verge of asking him something, but their relationship, it seemed, had not ripened to the point she felt comfortable saying what that thing might be. He was certain when it came it would not be an insignificant request, and he suspected he might be one of the few she thought capable of fulfilling it.

There was a way she looked at him, when she thought he wouldn't notice, that caused him to think of Tressa and her final treachery. He knew in his heart this witch woman was capable of much, much worse. He had no particular feelings for the woman and realized now that he must think only of himself if he was to get out of this country alive and with any hope of seeing Tressa again.

The woman did know healing. The blood no longer came when he coughed, and that little pain in his chest wasn't such a bother now. His arm was still not perfect, but it was better, and the poultice she had provided no doubt had helped.

Then too, there was the magic charm, the crystal that would make him invisible. How tantalizing the thought of this was to him, one who made his way in the world doing chancy things. The more he thought of it, the more he wondered if such a thing could possibly be true. And then, if she had the power to do such magic, what other evil things might she be capable of. Who could say what a witch might do should she set her mind to it. This was how Luca was thinking when he heard the far-off grind of the truck. The old man was coming.

~~~~~~~~

Sam's truck was well up the mountain and high enough to finally put them in range of Eldon Mayfield's radio. Charlie stared at the two-way as the FBI agent's voice crackled past the background static with enough punch to be understood, or nearly so. They could tell he was hot. "...what you're up...Sam...good reason." There was more than impatience in the words, and Samuel Shorthair lifted his brows and shot an unhappy glance at Charlie, who only shrugged and looked out the window. Sam shut the engine off, hoping that might make for better reception; still the voice faded in and out—a virtual static-storm of bits and snatches of conversation, some of them barely audible, while others were quite strong, though obviously from more distant parts of the reservation.

Charlie spoke first. "You know this is going to cost you with the bureau." He held up a finger and wagged it. "There's still time to turn around... This might be a wild goose chase anyway."

Samuel Shorthair said nothing, closed his eyes, and leaned back against the seat. "No, it's too late for that now. We'd best just go ahead on up there." He grinned over at Charlie. "That's the Indian talking, I guess. Not the FBI liaison officer."

Charlie grinned back but now wondered if they *were* making a mistake, and he had almost resolved to let Sam know that he too was having doubts when another truck came working its way down the nearly invisible ruts. There was no room to pass, and Samuel Short Hair bowed to local custom, giving way to the uphill vehicle by backing to the bare edge of the road. The old man driving saw the Navajo police emblem on the door of Sam's truck and slowly pulled abreast of them.

When the officer held up his hand the man stopped the vehicle and waited. Sam Shorthair got out and Charlie followed him over to the pickup, where the driver sat staring straight ahead. He obviously thought it best to let the "law" do the talking.

"*Yaa' eh t'eeh.*" Sam offered the usual Navajo salutation.

The old man looked at the pair and returned the greeting, but with little enthusiasm. "What can I help you with?" he asked in near perfect English, but directed the question to the only one of the two who appeared to be an actual policeman.

"Could I see some identification, please?" Sam looked past the driver and finished his usual cautious inspection of the vehicle's interior, then glanced into the bed of the truck, where he noted only a few empty cardboard boxes.

The old man dug out his wallet and handed over his driver's license. "What's this all about, if you don't mind me asking?"

Sam took the license and gave it his usual careful perusal, comparing the picture to the man, before handing it back. "Mr. Nez, we understand there's a …uh… woman living up the head of the canyon here and wondered if you had been up there this morning."

"Yes… her name is Margaret Hashkii. She's from Kiabito, but comes up here to gather medicine plants. I brought her in some supplies this morning. She's been coming up here for years." The old man retrieved the license from Sam and peered past him at Charlie, wondering if this person might be a fellow detainee. "She stays until early summer most years. I bring her in here quick as the snow goes off… deliver her groceries from time to time." The old man thought this pretty well covered everything the policeman could possibly want to know, and waited to hear if this was the case.

Sam spoke quietly and watched the man's reaction as he asked, "Is she alone up there this morning?" Without waiting for an answer, he asked, "Was anyone else around that you saw?"

"She's always alone. I've never seen anyone else up there, and didn't this time either."

The old man had developed an intermittent tick, first in one eye and then the other. Sam didn't think it unusual considering his age.

"She told me she would be through gathering the plants a little early this year," the man went on, deciding he was not through talking. "Said she has nearly enough of everything she needs now." Hosteen Nez pulled at one ear as though to help him think. "She wants me to come back for her next week, if there's not too much rain. You can't get back in here if it rains much."

Sam nodded and said, "We're with the search party looking for the person doing these killings they've had lately. I suppose you've heard about them, haven't you, sir? …We'd like to make sure everyone knows."

The old man nodded, narrowed his eyes at Sam as though he thought there might be more to it than that. "Oh yes," he said finally, "it's all over the news. They're warning everyone to be on the lookout. The woman knows, all right. I doubt there's anyone in this part of the country who doesn't know about the killings." He cocked an eye at Charlie and asked, "Are you a policeman too?"

Charlie spoke for the first time and assured him he was not. "I'm with Legal Services. I'm just helping out, volunteering, I guess you could say. We mainly just wanted to make sure the woman up there is all right and knows about the fugitive."

This seemed to satisfy the old man, and he turned back toward Samuel Shorthair. "If that's all you need from me, I need to get on my way. I've still got a long trip home."

"That should do it, Mr. Nez. Thanks for the information, and you have a safe trip."

The old man pulled past them, and without taking his eyes off the road, lifted an index finger in farewell. He didn't smile or look back.

Sam brought out a notebook and began jotting down the information from the form he'd filled in. "Arizona license... Man's name is Hosteen Nez. License says he's from Kaibito, all right." Sam's expression became pensive as he put away the notebook and stood looking after the retreating pickup. There was something bothering him about the old man, but he couldn't quite figure out what it was... and that bothered him even more.

"So what do you think, *hastiin*?" Charlie inclined his head in the direction of the truck. "Are you okay with what the old man told us, or do you still want to go take a look for yourself?" He smiled. "I'm good either way. Witches don't scare me."

Sam Shorthair looked at the ground and mulled it over before answering. "We're going up there."

They found they could drive within a hundred yards of the camp but had to go the rest of the way on foot. Thomas Begay had Charlie's .38, and Charlie had left the rifles borrowed from his Aunt Annie under the rear seat of his truck back at the highway, he figured Sam to be well enough armed for both of them.

Sam had his service revolver on his hip but at the last moment plucked the police-issue shotgun from its stand next to the center console, handed it to Charlie, and with a quick lift of his eyebrows, said, "You'll need to put one in the chamber... and I'd do it now."

Charlie nodded and jacked in a shell. "Double-ought buckshot?"

"Yep, deadliest load on the planet." Sam frowned. "You should carry one of those pumps in your truck."

Charlie hefted the scattergun. "I'm not called on to shoot many people in my job."

"Me neither, but ya just never know, now do you?"

As they moved closer to the camp, Charlie scanned the ground for tracks—his time with Harley and Thomas had, by now, made it almost second nature to look for sign. Sam was almost to the *hogan* door when Charlie stopped abruptly and gave a grunt of surprise. He pointed. "This hiking boot track is *his*," he said simply.

"What? The killer?" Sam had turned and now looked where Charlie was pointing. "Well, I'll be go to hell... are you sure?" Sam unsnapped the safety strap on his holster and lowered his voice. "Are you sure it couldn't have been old Hosteen Nez?"

"No, there are some smaller boot prints here. I noticed them when we parked the truck. I think they're the old man's. These others are the killer's, all right. I've been following them long enough; I should know." Both men quickly scanned the underbrush and looked long and hard at the ledges above the camp. Charlie Yazzie felt a sinking sensation in his stomach and grimaced. "I doubt he's still out there, or one of us would already have a bullet in him."

Sam pulled his service revolver and eased up to one side of the *hogan* door while Charlie raised the shotgun and covered him. Sam hesitated only a moment before throwing open the blanket at the entrance. He counted to ten and, with clenched jaw and revolver at the ready, entered the dim interior.

Charlie waited nearly a minute before calling out, "You okay in there?" A minute is a long time under those circumstances, but still he wasn't quite ready to follow Sam in.

When he did come out, Sam's face was as grey as an Indian's face can be, and he sucked in an audible breath before murmuring, "Well, I guess that old myth about witches being bullet-proof doesn't hold water." It was clear Sam was shaken, but he maintained his game-face when he looked Charlie in the eye. "Looks like she was first shot from a distance, and from up high. It was a poor shot—he had to come down and finish her with a knife. It was after that she was dragged into her *hogan*."

Charlie moved to the door and peered in. After his eyes adjusted to the gloom of the interior, he saw what must be Margaret Hashkii, face up on a layer of sheepskins and clearly shot in the shoulder by a large caliber rifle. Charlie could easily see the deep slashes across her midsection, mute evidence of the power behind the blade. Behind him, Sam Shorthair peeked over his shoulder and said he figured she'd been dead less than two hours—possibly even less. She might even have been dead by the time old Hosteen Nez had arrived with the groceries. There was a backpack leaned against the far wall, and Charlie went over to it, studied it in the dim light, but before he could touch it, Sam spoke from the glare of the doorway and waved a finger back and forth, "I wouldn't do that, Charlie. The FBI's hell on no one disturbing the crime scene."

Charlie didn't like it and inclined his head in such a manner Sam could see he didn't like it. After a few moments contemplation he said, "I'm fairly certain that's the backpack taken from the first victim. It fits the description, according to what the backpacker's wife told the FBI."

Sam was adamant. "I know it does. I read the report too, but we have to leave it for the feds."

Charlie shook his head. "There could be something important in there... might help us right now." Charley knew this was flying in the face of his own admonishments to Thomas and Harley, but things were different now. He wanted this guy to go down, and he wanted it to be at the hands of the Navajo Nation. He sighed finally and shook his head. "But I'm going to defer to your judgment as the official investigating officer, and leave it be."

Sam didn't like it either, "We're already in enough trouble with the FBI and I don't want to risk a full-blown shitstorm." He changed the subject. "Didn't it seem a little strange to you that Hosteen Nez didn't get out of the truck when he pulled up. Most people around here do... And then he just kept on talking, telling us things we hadn't even asked about. Most people in this country are pretty close-mouthed when it comes to talking to the law, especially old people."

Charlie reflected back. "No, I hadn't thought about it 'til you mentioned it, but I can see what you're saying." Charlie pointed to the backpack. "I do know one thing—that gear being left here tells me he no longer needs it... and he's not coming back. He's gone, Sam. We missed him."

"Well if he doesn't need his gear, did he walk out of here? It's a long way to the highway on foot."

"He's not on foot, Sam. He was in Hosteen Nez's pickup truck."

Sam snorted, "He wasn't in that truck—it was a single cab, and you saw me check the interior and even the bed... a few old cardboard boxes was all there was in it."

"Sam, that truck was the same model as that old government truck I used to have. There's a pretty healthy storage space behind the seat, for tools and such. Remember when that tourist-lady turned up missing in the campground over at Kayenta? That's where they found her, in a space just like that, when they stopped her husband the next day down in Shiprock. The man looked so harmless and in such distress over his wife's disappearance that it didn't occur to anyone to look behind the seat."

Sam bumped his forehead with the palm of his hand. "I remember hearing about that and wondering where he'd hid the body in a single cab truck, especially one that had already been through two check points. Everyone thought she had been kidnapped... She was no midget, either, as I recall."

"If that's how it is, we better get a move on." Charlie indicated Margaret Hashkii's body with a nod of his head. "You'll have to call this in on the go... assuming we can get out on the radio."

Charlie's mind was filled with possible scenarios as they raced to the truck, buckled up, and braced themselves for the treacherous downhill run. Sam spun the unit around and gunned it downhill, barely missing assorted rocks and small junipers.

*This has to be it*, Charlie thought. *It's the only possible thing that makes any sense.*

Sam gripped the wheel with both hands and was jumping gullies they had previously only crept across on the way up. It was a nearly new truck, but Charlie knew it couldn't take the pounding Sam was handing out, not without breaking something. That could mean big trouble.

Immediately Sam seemed to channel Charlie's cautionary thoughts and slowed the truck considerably. Still, Charlie thought his driving was on the edge. When Sam glanced over at the Legal Services investigator, he saw him clutching the pump shotgun tight to his chest, eyes wide, and feet braced, and taking this as a cautionary indicator, slowed the vehicle even more, causing Charlie to relax his grip on the shotgun somewhat. Sam hoped the gun's safety was on. Charlie had never ejected the live shell in the chamber that he could recall.

Fleetingly, Charlie wished Harley and Thomas were there. They each had more reason to be in at the kill than him. Then thought, *What the hell is wrong with me? Why would I want my two best friends here, where they might very likely get shot?* He could see Sam gritting his teeth as he manhandled the truck, still barely keeping it on the road. From time to time and even at this lower speed, the truck threatened to plunge off the edge.

Sam swung wide to navigate a treacherous corner and thought for a moment he had lost it. He wrestled with the wheel and managed to straighten the truck in the new direction. As they came about, Samuel Shorthair's eyes widened and he hit the brake pedal.

Charlie, too, couldn't help but suck in his breath at the sight of Hosteen Nez's blue pickup, crosswise of the road, a rifle across the hood, and behind the rifle the devil incarnate. Though they were still a good distance away, Charlie knew instantly and without doubt who the shooter was, and what was about to happen. "Look out!" he choked as he lurched to one side and threw his arms up to cover his face. Sam Short-hair instantly swerved the truck, but not in time to avoid the heavy lead bullet that came smashing through the windshield. The truck ran itself partially up the embankment before lurching to a stop against a juniper tree.

Charlie, when at last he became aware of his surroundings, was partially propped up against a front wheel. He could feel the rough treads of the tire against his back and mentally checked himself over before opening his eyes. He thought he was going to be all right—felt surprisingly little pain—certainly not pain of the caliber he had expected; he was fairly certain that would come eventually. He was careful when he opened his eyes, afraid things might be worse than he thought… and they were.

The *mojado* squatted just in front of him, with what might pass for a concerned look on his face. His rifle, at half cock, lay across his knees, and he rocked back on his heels as he contemplated his adversary.

"You not hurt too bad? No?" He watched Charlie intently. "Don' you die on me now, you *cabron*." Concern was indeed evident in his voice as he reached out and gently shook Charlie's shoulder. "You one a those Indios who been following me, no?" He squinted one eye, half-smiled, and knew it was so. "I think you one of 'em, all right. I think you the one always draggin' ass behind them other two. You shouldn' let that lil' fat one get ahead… make you look weak, *hombre*." He held up Charlie's badge. "You a policeman? You don' got no special shirt… You don' got no gun… but, you got this badge *hombre*. How is that, *amigo?* How you come by this badge?" He turned the badge over and over and polished it a little with his hand, holding it to the light of a darkening sky. He attempted to read the inscription, but it was beyond him, and finally he could only shake his head at the unfamiliar words.

Charlie stared back and thought carefully before he spoke. There was the chance his life just might hang on it. "I'm not a policeman. I work in an office. I was just out here helping look for some cattle."

"Well, then why you followin' me, *hombre*?" He shrugged. "I don' got you cows." He looked up and down the road as though to assure Charlie there were no cattle. "I don' know nothin' 'bout no cows. *Pero...* what I do know, is you not gonna get off so easy, like you other *compadre*." He grimaced. "You save him a good cuttin' that night, *amigo...* How he's doin' now? He don' die from bein' too scared, huh?" He smiled at his little joke. "Don' you worry, my friend. I won' cut you. I think I gonna need you pretty quick."

Charlie's nose hurt, and when he tried to touch it, it seemed oddly off center on his face. That's when he became aware of the handcuffs—Sam Shorthair's handcuffs. But he couldn't see Sam and assumed he was still in the truck. He didn't hold out much hope for his friend—It had been a solid hit. There is a different, almost hollow, sort of thump when a large caliber bullet hits the chest cavity. Charlie had hunted enough as a boy to know it when he heard it. He had always liked Sam, and now, he too, had a reason to hate. There is a vast disparity in the lexicon between dislike and hate, and what Charlie felt now was the latter, quite possibly the strongest of human emotions.

"*Como se llama?* What you name *esse*? I need somethin' to call you. *Me llama* es Luca," he said by way of illustration.

"Charlie, my name is Charlie," the investigator whispered. "What do you want from me?"

"Well... for a long time I jus' want you people to leave me alone, you know, get off my ass. *Pero, ahorita* I gonna need a lil' help... and you the only one left to do it. That old man over there by the *trucke*... he's dead now. I thought maybe he could drive me where I want to go, but when I have him pull the truck across the road, he jump out and make a run for it... He was fast, too, for an old man. *Puta!* He damn near make it to the trees. If I had time, I woulda' run him down... but then I hear you *trucke* comin' ...an I jus' end it. Crazy ol' *cabron*... he shoulda' know'd he couldn' outrun no bullet." And when Luca shrugged, there was no remorse at all in it.

"So what now?" Charlie needed time to think—he would be in league with the devil, he knew, but that was the cost of the thing, and there was no help for it as far as he could see. On the wild ride down the mountain, he'd had time to try the radio only twice, and he doubted much of it had gotten out; he'd heard no answer beyond a garbled static. The search party would have already gone out, including FBI Agent Eldon Mayfield and his two new field agents. They were headed up high, Sam had said, so he expected the chances of running into any of them this low on the mountain were probably slim to none. Sam's patrol unit was now out of action, and he doubted this Luca Tarango, if that was his name, would have wanted to call that much attention to himself anyhow. That left the old man's truck, and until his body was found and the alert put out, it would be the only reasonable option. In the end, however, Charlie knew this man would decide he needed another vehicle.

Luca stared down the road for a moment and, as though reading Charlie's thoughts, said, "*No me gusta este trucke viejo,*" and then remembering who he was talking to, translated, "I don' like that old *trucke*. It only goes slow an' it smokes a bunch a smoke. No, the cops will stop it sooner or later, an' there we be. We need a better *trucke*—*mas major*— –if we going to get where I need to go."

"We? Where do you want *us* to go?" Charlie wanted desperately to make some sort of connection—information in

Charlie's law enforcement manual considered it crucial in hostage situations. "Why do you need me?"

*"Colorado."* Luca said this with the Spanish pronunciation, just as the conquistadors must have said it in the beginning. "Oh... an' I don' drive... not like you drive in this country." Luca didn't want to admit he didn't know how to read, road signs or otherwise. He was smart enough to know the slightest driving error could be his downfall. Driving was out of the question for one of his slight experience. No, he would need help.

A spark of hope was stirring in Charlie, and he considered the possibilities. Should the man be persuaded to take *his* truck, it might open up a few possibilities. It was still parked at the highway department turnoff, which is where he had told Thomas and Harley he would leave it if he hooked up with Sam Shorthair. He seriously doubted any searchers would come straggling in until late afternoon. Many of the volunteers' vehicles should still be there to choose from. The trick would be to convince his captor to take *his* truck and not some other.

Luca came to his feet, reached down to grab the chain connecting the cuffs, and pulled his prisoner to his feet. A wave of dizziness rolled over Charlie when he came upright. The first thing he saw was Sam Shorthair, still in the truck, slumped over the wheel—and apparently lifeless.

Charlie gritted his teeth as he was dragged along past Sam's vehicle and the short distance to Hosteen Nez's pickup. There was something wrong with his knee, and he favored it noticeably. He could see the old man's boots sticking out of the bushes at the edge of the clearing. He couldn't help but think of the anguish the old man must have felt as he talked to Sam Shorthair earlier that morning, knowing there was a gun pointed at his back and every word was being weighed. Charlie knew now that Sam's premonition had been right when he thought something not quite right about the old man. Navajo cops like Sam Shorthair didn't come along every day.

Luca motioned for Charlie to go ahead of him to the body, where the two of them dragged the limp form further into the underbrush and out of sight. Once back at the old man's truck, the *mojado* indicated Charlie was to take the wheel, but only when he was seated on the other side did he pass him the key. Charlie held the handcuffs out to him and questioned silently with his eyes. The fugitive shook his head no, and pointed to the shift lever. It was an automatic, and he indicated with a nod of his chin that Charlie could handle it.

Charlie did not lower the cuffs, but made them jingle, and insisted, "What if we get stopped? These cuffs won't look too good."

The fugitive grinned. "If we get stopped, Mr. Charlie, you gonna be dead anyway. They know who they look'n for."

Luca Tarango had been right in his assessment of the truck. It was slow, even slower up hill, and it did smoke a lot. It looked like they were purposely laying a trail of fog all the way down the mountain.

# 18

## *The Search*

Harley Ponyboy thought they had done well. Word had spread like a brush fire among his clan members, and their two missing horses were found only a few miles from where they had been turned loose. The saddles and gear had also been recovered, and the Natanii sheep company had been more than accommodating in their efforts to bring everything together and transport it down to the trailhead, where Clyde was to pick up the two of them later in the afternoon.

Harley was told his clan mother, She Has Horses, was now with her sister and nephew, where she was trying to re-weave the threads of her life. She would, for the first time in many years, be a closer part of her maternal family, and while she would always have a place there, it would not be the same as when she'd had a family of her own. Harley told his clansmen he would try to get by to see the old woman and let her know how things were progressing in regard to catching the person responsible for her granddaughter's death. He knew there was little he could say or do to ease her mind, but at the same time, felt any effort would be appreciated and might even contribute to the general effort to restore *hozo* to the clan.

Thomas Begay, too, had held up well during a day that Harley expected might take a toll on his weakened condition. The two sat in the shade of a small copse of spruce trees near the trailhead corrals. Charlie and Thomas's horses nibbled at the young cheat-grass battling its way through the clumps of manure left in the pens.

Thomas played with the end of a rope, coiling it and tossing it toward a rock. "I'll bet Charlie hooked up with Sam Shorthair and he's talked him into looking in on that witch-woman up Little Water Canyon." He said this in such a manner that Harley took it to mean Thomas himself, had he been in Charlie's place, would have done things differently.

"I guess you are probably right, considering neither one of them probably had any idea what else ta do." Harley watched Thomas fling the rope out well beyond the target, then snake the loop over the rock with a little twist of the wrist as he retrieved it. Thomas could do some magical things with a rope, and Harley envied him that. "Charlie and Sam Shorthair better be careful up there. Neither one knows much about witches." He sighed and fixed Thomas with a frown. "We shoulda' waited ta get these horses. We coulda' gone on with Charlie instead of foolin' around here all day." He didn't exactly intimate that it was Thomas's fault they hadn't gone with Charlie, but still Thomas got that impression.

"Well, I think he maybe didn't want us there anyway... I think maybe he figured the FBI would be more likely to accept him if he didn't drag us along." Thomas chuckled. "Charlie probably thinks being with Sam Shorthair will make him part of the "official" investigation and not just out there poking around." This hadn't actually occurred to Harley, and he frowned as he considered the probability of the thing. It was about this time they saw Clyde's new Dodge truck racing across the flats below the mountain and heading their way.

The recent rains had laid the dust down, and there was no mistake who was coming. Still, Harley shaded his eyes with one hand and made positive identification. "It's Clyde, all right, and he's got Annie's new horse trailer on behind."

"I wouldn't expect any less," Thomas smiled. "Don't kid yourself. That truck's Annie's too. Everything's still in her name, from what I hear. Charlie's Aunt Annie is smart, and she's watched enough cop shows that she's got a pretty good fix on where Clyde's coming from."

Clyde started blowing the horn long before he pulled up, and the two men gathered their gear and readied the horses to load.

Clyde's first words on climbing down out of the pickup were, "Did you see any cows with our brand?"

Thomas looked him up and down, started to say something harsh, but then allowed for the fact that the man *was* Annie Eagletree's husband. "We did see a few with *Annie's* brand on 'em but didn't fool with 'em. They were headed back down country anyway."

Clyde let the insinuation regarding ownership of the cows go by without comment but made a mental note not to take Thomas on as a hired hand in the future. Had Thomas known Clyde's decision in advance, he would have dealt with the "cattle baron" on a different level. These little banty roosters needed the occasional attitude adjustment, in his view. Everyone liked Annie Eagletree, and most thought this little man was taking advantage of her in some ways.

After the horses were loaded and the three men were once again on their way out to the highway, Clyde hooked a thumb over his shoulder at the cooler on the back seat. "Annie made some more sandwiches, and I put a few beers underneath should you want something to drink." He knew the two no longer drank and smiled when he made the offer. Harley cut his eyes at Clyde, reached back, and came up with two sandwiches, one of which he offered to Thomas.

"Pass me one of those beers, Harley," Clyde said, grinning.

Harley knew what the man was doing, and while it rankled, he said nothing. He just reached back, pulled a beer from the cooler, and handed it to Clyde.

Thomas looked around Harley and said, "I can drive if you want, Clyde. This time a day there's going to be some cops out."

Clyde brushed it aside. "Don't you worry, my man. I'll do the driving. … And, I'll let you know should I not feel up to it." It was said that Clyde grew more eloquent of speech as he drank, and some attributed this to his mother, who was a high-school teacher and quite well thought of in Farmington's white community. She belonged to several ladies groups, and this caused talk on the reservation, some going so far as to call her an "apple."

Thomas figured Clyde already had a few on his way up. They were going a little faster than he thought wise on this back road, and he was concerned about how the horses were riding in the trailer.

After they swerved onto the highway and had probably gone no more than a mile, there came the chirp of a siren, and Thomas looked in the side mirror to see the flashing lights of a Navajo police unit.

Harley stared straight ahead but couldn't suppress a grin. "Looks like you got company back there, Clyde. Better find a place to pull over. I doubt you can outrun him with this horse trailer on."

Clyde checked his mirror, scowled, and handed Harley the beer, who passed it to Thomas, who looked at it only a moment before throwing the near empty can in the glove box and clicking the latch. He knew that probably wouldn't help, but it was all he could do. He was glad now that he'd put Charlie's revolver in a saddlebag back in the horse trailer's tack compartment.

By the time officer Billy Red Clay was at the door, Clyde had rolled down the window and was making shooing motions with his hands. He pointed to the air conditioner, and Harley turned it on.

"How are you boys today?" Billy smiled. He knew each of them and their reputations to boot. He and Thomas were of the same clan and not so distantly related.

"Oh, we're fine," Clyde mumbled, not looking directly at the officer.

"Clyde, did you not see that stop sign, coming up onto the highway? It's a big one."

Clyde scratched his chin and pretended to think about it. "I could have missed it—there was a bee got in the truck about that time, and I was trying to shoo him out."

Harley continued staring out the front window, but Thomas smiled across and lifted a finger to the officer. He'd known Billy since he was a baby and had been disappointed when he learned the young man had chosen this particular career path.

"Clyde, could you step out of the vehicle, and bring some ID with you." It wasn't a question. Billy Red Clay was wearing his official face.

"You know who I am, Billy. You just stopped me last week..." Clyde immediately wished he hadn't said that part, and fumbled for his wallet.

"I know Clyde... that's what concerns me." Billy leafed through his citation book. "I let you go with a warning last week, and now I'm afraid my generosity didn't make much of an impression."

Harley elbowed Thomas, and both men were grinning when Officer Red Clay told Clyde to step out of the vehicle for the second time.

Harley knew there were people who had never been stopped by an officer of the law and didn't understand the protocol, but Clyde wasn't in that group, and neither was he or Thomas. "Do you want us to get out, too, Billy?

"No, you two boys just stay in the truck." And then addressed Harley. "Me and Thomas are both 'Bitter Water' clan... I doubt he'll shoot me... I doubt you will either,

Harley." He added this last part after a reflective pause, and mostly as a courtesy, Harley thought.

Clyde sighed, took the clip-on insurance card off the sun visor, and exited the vehicle.

Billy Red Clay got right up in Clyde's face and said, "I believe I smell alcohol, Clyde. You haven't been drinking, have you? I mean, right here on the reservation—you'd know better than that, wouldn't you, Clyde?" He shook his head as he started a new form on his citation pad. "I'm afraid you're going to have to blow a test for me, Clyde."

Clyde's shoulders sagged, then straightened as he drew himself to his full height, and though he only came to Billy Red Clay's shoulder, he affected a belligerent manner, which he was known to do when hard pressed. He said, "Now you look here, Billy Red Clay, I'm not blowing into a damn thing!"

Inside the truck, Harley nudged Thomas again and chuckled.

The tribal officer put Clyde up against the fender, patted him down, then had him put his hands behind his back to receive a zip tie.

Billy looked into the truck. "Either one of you boys still have a driver's license?"

"I don't," Harley admitted, "but Thomas here does... He got it back almost a year ago." Harley had always been good about volunteering Thomas's information to the law. He had, several times in the past, helped police fill out Thomas's arrest papers when Thomas was too drunk to do it himself.

Billy Red Clay was looking at Thomas when he said, "Uncle, how about you and Harley taking Annie's truck back to her. You can tell her, I'm going to run Clyde into Shiprock and put him in holding until I get the okay for his blood test." He then addressed the prisoner one final time, "Clyde, you could save yourself a lot of trouble if you just blow in the machine for me."

"Nope, I'm not going to do it." Clyde had set his jaw, and everyone could see there was no changing his mind.

"Alrighty then, let's go. But Clyde, don't think stalling for time is going to help you. These new tests factor all those things in." Billy Red Clay's normally ruddy complexion was a shade darker by the time he got Clyde stuffed into the back seat of the cruiser.

The policeman came back to the truck just as Thomas started the engine. "I was going to mention... I think I heard Charlie on the radio earlier. I was at the end of my run down to Dinnehotso and could only make out a few words. He sounded a little excited—something about a witch... or maybe he was in the ditch... something. Anyway, I didn't hear any more after that so figured he had things sorted out."

~~~~~~~

Annie Eagletree, when later told what happened, cussed for a full five minutes, and during that time, let it be known she wasn't going to bail Clyde out. She'd wasted enough of her money, and her nephew's time, on Clyde's behalf. "Charlie has more important things to do," she said, "than running around making bail for drunks and getting them out of jail." But she was not through. "By hell, Clyde better just get his credit established down there at the police station, if that's where he means to spend his time."

When they finally got Annie Eagletree settled down, it was drawing well onto evening. Thomas let her re-bandage his head and give him his third shot of Combiotic, and then, as he pulled up his pants, asked could he leave their horses in the corral... and borrow her truck to go see what had become of Charlie. He said her nephew should be back at the search outpost and waiting for them by now. He didn't mention what Billy Red Clay had said regarding what he'd heard on the radio, but he had a bad feeling in the pit of his stomach each time he thought of it.

"Sure," Annie said, "you boys go on and take that truck. You can't be any harder on it than Clyde is."

Before they left, Thomas asked if he could use the phone, and went into the other room to make sure no one heard.

Once back on the road, Thomas winced when he tried to find a comfortable position in the driver's seat."

Harley, ever solicitous, asked, "Where did she give you the shot this time?"

Thomas frowned. "Right on top of the first one."

"Ouch! That must have hurt some, but you know, you only have two butt halves, so it had to go somewhere." Harley was the master of the obvious; most had come to consider it just his way of making conversation. "How you feeling now?" Harley went on. "Those stitches starting to pull a little, are they?"

"I'm okay. My head don't hurt at all… only my butt." Thomas's mind was elsewhere—wondering what Charlie had been talking about on the two way, if it had even been him on the radio. Thomas was now convinced Harley was right, they should have forgotten about the horses that morning and just stuck with Charlie.

At the highway department pull-off there was only Charlie's truck and one other left in the parking lot; the other being a beat up brown Toyota with the hood up, obviously broken down.

To the west of the Carrizos it was beginning to look like rain. The spiraling black thunderheads built to an anvil top, collided, then tumbled over one another—thin veins of lightning skittered about the edges and lit the red cliffs in a way one usually only sees in the movies. Thomas pulled up next to Charlie's truck and Harley got out, cupped his hands to the window, and peered in. After a few seconds he looked back at Thomas and gave a lift of his shoulders. "Doesn't look like he's been back all day. The sandwich Annie packed him this morning is still on the seat and so is his thermos. He musta gone off with someone else."

Thomas pondered this for a moment and then climbed down from Annie's truck and went over to see for himself. "I see the butt end of one of those rifles he borrowed from Annie. It's sticking out from under the rear seat." He seemed surprised. "It's a wonder someone hasn't broken in and stolen it." And then he said, "Probably no one wants to mess with a official vehicle. But eventually someone will come along who will." In that part of the country, leaving any sign of a gun in a vehicle was like leaving a stack of cash on the seat. It hadn't been like that when Thomas was young, but that was back when everyone already had a gun. People seemed a lot more polite then and less likely to steal... for some reason.

Harley went around to the front of the truck, got down on one knee, and felt around under the bumper for the little magnetic key box Charlie "hid" his emergency key in. "Him and Sam Shorthair musta' gone off together. If he went with the rest of the searchers, he would have been back by now." Harley came back and handed Thomas the key. "We might as well take those guns. They're not doing anyone any good here. Might keep them from getting stole, too."

Thomas opened the door and pulled out the rifles, then handed Harley several boxes of the ammunition that was stacked behind them. "Charlie must have been expecting quite a little shootout," he said, noting the rather generous amount of rifle fodder. "That's usually not like him, but maybe he's getting better sense in his old age."

Harley smiled to himself as they removed the armaments and put them in Annie's truck. Thomas went back and got the sandwich and thermos. "There's no use in letting this go to waste either," he said tearing the sandwich in two and handing Harley half. "Do you think we'd better go ask that woodcutter kid, up the road, how to get to Little Water Canyon? Charlie's got the topo map—I've no idea where the turnoff is."

Harley munched on his portion of the sandwich. "Lester Hoskinni?"

"Yes, dammit Harley, Lester Hoskinni. How many woodcutters have we run across up here?" Thomas's butt hurt, and it was making him irritable.

Harley frowned. "There is no need ta get testy, Thomas. How's your butt?"

Thomas grimly shook his head, sighed, and said, "...Fine, Harley... just fine." His mood was dark and he rubbed his chin and wondered out loud, "I'm thinking now we should hang around here a bit longer; Charlie could still show up...and it might be a good idea to check his two-way first; see what the word on the street is. There has to be some chatter out there. Besides, I know he'll be back for his truck eventually... if he's all right... and if not, there's little we can do about it right now. We have no idea where he or Sam Shorthair really are, or how to go about finding them." Thomas was right, of course, but surprised at how cold this sounded. Even Harley looked taken aback.

"Well, we have to do something!" Harley was incensed. "According to what Billy Red Clay heard on the radio, Charlie could be off in a ditch somewhere and need help getting out... might be hurt, for all we know." Harley was generally prone to optimism regardless how hard the facts of a matter appeared. In this case, however, he knew Thomas was probably right. There really wasn't much they could do. "I think we better check with Lester Hoskinni and see what he knows."

# 19

## *The Storm*

Luca Tarango stared in disgust at the trucks front wheel—splayed out at an impossible angle. "You tol' me you could drive," he said accusingly.

"No... you told me I *had* to drive." Charlie Yazzie put his hands to his face and rubbed his eyes, making the chain on the cuffs jingle, then pushed his chin toward the front end. "The tie-rod's broken. Wouldn't have mattered who was driving... it would have broke."

The *mojado* looked again at the wheel and shrugged, then turned his gaze down the forest service road, and toward the highway he knew was down there. "How far ta the big road?"

"...Not sure, seven, eight miles, maybe... maybe farther." Charlie could smell the rain coming, and judging from the towering black thunderheads to the west, it was going to be a good one. In a couple of hours, it wouldn't matter what kind of truck they had—even his four-wheel drive would have a tough time of it on the mountain then.

"We don' got no food, no blankets... and a broken *trucke*." The man said these things as though bringing them to the fore would clarify the situation—possibly even suggest a solution. He didn't seem angry or even frustrated, and as far as Charlie could tell, none of this seemed to bother him in the least. It was almost as if he considered this sort of bad luck the norm and not worth dwelling on.

The fact was, it really *didn't* matter to Luca. This was how life was. It was like the ocean—there was an ebb and flow to it. Sometimes the current was against you, and sometimes not. The important thing was to never quit trying, not because you expected anything good to come of it, but rather for the certainty of what would happen if you didn't.

Charlie was beginning to see a glimmer of how the man's mind worked and became even more certain he was in a very dangerous position indeed. Thomas and Harley were out there somewhere—looking for him, most likely. He had that, at least. Someone who cared was close, and that alone was enough to fuel hope. He looked at the man across from him and wondered what it would be like to have no one who really cared. He didn't feel sorry for the man, or any less likely to take him down if he got the chance, still there was a feeling of emptiness that any person should come to so sorry a life.

The Mexican studied the sky, judged the wind, and came to a reasonably accurate forecast for the remainder of the day; dark and gloomy, with more rain than the rutted road could handle was his private opinion—almost immediately the thought became a self-fulfilling prophesy.

The storm, when it came, brought with it a cold wind before the deluge. After only a mile in the thick clay mud, it was all Charlie could do to put one foot in front of the other. The *mojado,* behind him, rifle at the ready, slogged along immersed in a world Charlie couldn't even imagine. Luca's life growing up had been nothing like Charlie's. There had been beatings, both from older boys, and his father, who felt there was something odd about him right from the start. Eventually everyone realized what it was that set him apart, and then they feared him and left him alone. He had always been different, smarter in some ways, crueler in others. Different.

At that moment, the *mojado* was thinking only of the mud. *In the hands of someone who knew what he was doing, this mud might make good adobe bricks. Not the equal of those in my village, of course, but serviceable nonetheless.* When his attention returned to the work at hand, he knew most likely he would have to do more killing, but that was what he did best. No matter that it might be a child, or a woman, or even a dog—should it occur to him it was needed—he would do it, and think no more of it than swatting a fly.

Charlie suspected they were not far from the turnoff to the designated woodcutting area, the one used by the Hoskinni family. He fervently hoped young Lester Hoskinni had the good sense to quit early and already be on his way down the mountain. He studied the road in front of him but could not make out any conclusive indicators that this was the case. The ruts of the road had become torrents of foaming brown water and it would be impossible for anyone to get up this road now, and probably for several days to come. He couldn't help but consider what might drive a man like Luca. It was more of a professional interest than anything else and at one point he thought to ask him why he had killed the witch-woman... or the old man for that matter, but then thought better of it. He was on thin enough ice already, and who knew what might bring him to even more violence.

Charlie seemed to recall a point of rock somewhere just ahead that might offer some shelter until the worst of the storm passed. He thought he remembered a blow-down of spruce just in front of a rock overhang. It couldn't be far, less than a mile he guessed. He was an excellent judge of distance and only hoped he could hold out that long. When Sam Shorthair's truck had rammed the embankment, he had apparently jammed one knee. Now it was beginning to pain, and threatened to give way beneath him. He seriously doubted his captor would greet such a development with any degree of sympathy.

Luca Tarango watched with some curiosity as Charlie trudged along through the mud in front of him. He noticed him favoring his right leg slightly. Something he had noticed previously but judged to be not so serious. That could prove a problem should it grow worse. He had first thought the rain would not last and the storm would soon pass over them—meaning they might reach the highway before full dark. Now, however, he thought differently. The main brunt of the thunderheads had moved past but in their wake had left a steady rain from the southwest. He could smell the wet mesquite up from Mexico, and it was a balm to his spirit. He felt strong, surprised at how much better off he seemed than this younger person. Perhaps the man really did work in an office as he had maintained. That made more sense to him now that he thought about it. A plan had come together in his head, and this man with a badge was to be part of it. He would make certain allowances with that in mind, but in the end would do what he had to do to survive, and if that meant changing the plan, so be it. As he was thinking this through, he saw Charlie hesitate, stop, and look uphill to a ridge and rocky outcrop—only a few hundred feet off the track, but barely visible through the driving rain.

Charlie saw the *mojado* raise the rifle slightly and thought for a moment he had decided to shoot him. When that didn't happen, he pointed to the rocks. "There's shelter up there behind that down timber. Let's get out of this rain for a while… at least until it lets up a little."

The *mojado* silently considered this, stared at Charlie a moment, and then motioned with the rifle barrel that Charlie was to lead the way. There was an overhang in the rock wall, sheltered from the wind by dead timber. It was nearly dry under the outcrop, almost calm compared to the wind-driven downpour outside, and both men paused to breathe after the short climb.

"Fire?" Charlie questioned, pointing at the abundant supply of dry wood within easy reach.

Luca turned and looked out toward the road, but he couldn't even see it from here. He nodded. "*Si… como que no?*" There was no reason not to. No one would be on the road in this weather.

Charlie was now trembling from the cold and wet. He quickly collected a bundle of dry twigs and small branches, which he piled at the front of the shelter. He saw the *mojado* take out a small plastic vial of the sort back-packers use for their matches. Soon they had a respectable fire going and began feeding it larger pieces of wood. The heat bounced off the rock wall—enough heat that their clothes steamed, and eventually began to dry. They sat with their backs against the rock wall, luxuriating in the warmth of the blaze.

Charlie saw that the handcuffs were wearing raw rings around his wrists and looked over at the man sprawled beside him, rifle still aimed in his general direction. "How about it?" he asked, holding up the cuffs.

The *mojado* tilted his head and smiled, then shook his head. "I don' think so, *hombre*. We not that good a friends yet… No, I don' think so, Mr. Charlie."

Both were silent then, one or the other occasionally feeding a twig or two to the fire, both growing drowsy as they warmed and darkness came upon them.

Luca dozed intermittently, but only for short periods, waking with a start each time to check his prisoner. When awake, Luca thought only of *Tressa,* and when he dozed he dreamed only of her. Even when awake and trying to figure out what his next move should be, his thoughts returned to the woman. Dreams of people he had harmed never bothered him. He had long ago learned to block those things from his subconscious. In truth he was as barren of such memories as the most innocent of children. Charlie had fallen asleep almost instantly, while the *mojado* watched and envied him that little luxury.

About midnight the rain stopped. As night moved toward morning, the pain in Charlie's knee increased, finally waking him in the wee hours. The thought of his wife and son came to him then, as it did each morning before dawn.

There was the bittersweet vision of their little place with its garden and corrals. The strangling thought he might never see them again temporarily overwhelmed him. Home and family was what it was all about. Never had they seemed so dear as now, on the brink of what might well be his last hours. These were maudlin thoughts, he knew, and he shook his head to clear his brain—the future of his family depended on what he did next... And not only them. There was the very real chance this man would kill again—there were others to consider.

Charlie opened one eye, just a crack, saw the *mojado*, eyes wide, staring blankly into the misty dawn. Charlie thought he heard something, and while it might have been part of a dream or other figment of his imagination, he came instantly alert but gave no outward sign. What the sound had been, he could not now say; only that it was something out of tune with the night. As he lay perfectly still, he listened... Soon, there it was again... It was something very faint and far away. From under an eyelid he watched Luca Tarango and saw no indication the man had heard anything. This was not the first time Charlie suspected the man's hearing was not good.

He listened intently now, concentrating every fiber of his being on identifying the slightest out-of-place sound. Finally, there was no doubt in his mind that it was the sound of an engine still several miles distant, definitely louder now than when he first heard it. He shot a quick glance at the Mexican and still saw no sign that he had heard. He continued to listen as the sound became more distinct—the struggle of a truck, clawing its way up the mountain. Just as he thought it must surely attract the attention of his captor, it died away.

The *mojado*'s eyes signaled nothing and he was, it seemed, still lost in his own thoughts. But then slowly he turned and his hollow eyes reflected the notion that something was not as it should be.

Charlie looked away wincing as he tried to straighten his leg. The knee had tightened during the night; it was only with some effort that he was able to gain his feet and stand supported by the wall behind him. Luca observed the process with a certain detached interest, then arose and, setting his rifle against a rock, stirred the ashes of the fire, added a few broken branches to the coals, and watched as they ignited, the glow more an illusion of warmth than actual heat.

Charlie rustled around, breaking more wood, adding it to the fire. Noise, he thought, might prevent the truck from being heard, should it happen to start up again.

"Why you want so big a fire?" Luca frowned. "We not going to be here that long, *amigo*. You leg hurt you maybe? You not able to walk good this morning?" There was disappointment in his voice, but Charlie knew the concern was not for him, but rather for the strategy he had become part of.

"I'll be fine, once I start moving around… Knee just stiffened up. It'll be okay in a few minutes."

"I hope so, Mr. Charlie. I would not like to leave you here by you ownself. Something bad maybe happen to you then." He nodded, looking into the fire. "I don' want to loose you now after all this trouble."

Charlie caught the implication in the words, and it sent a chill down his back the fire couldn't dispel and he thought, *this knee better improve quickly. We need to move out. This shelter is not easily approachable without being seen and someone is coming.* Of that he was certain.

They worked their way back down to the road, Charlie slipping occasionally in the mud and silently cursing each time his leg threatened to give way. It wasn't any better by time they came to the road, worse in fact; the *mojado* looked grim as he watched. Charlie could see why the truck had stopped. The rutted track had become a quagmire, impassible even for a 4-wheel drive. He estimated they were still more than a mile from where he thought he'd last heard the laboring truck. If it were Thomas and Harley, they would not be just sitting there in a disabled truck. There was enough light now to move. Hunting light, his grandfather called it.

Charlie hummed to himself… louder as they went along.

"*Oyea!*" The *mojado* tapped Charlie on the shoulder with the muzzle of the rifle. "Shut up, *hombre*! What the hell's a matter with you, *cabron*?" He growled, "You makin' it real hard for me to like you, sonofabitch. Maybe I gonna have to kill you now. You no gonna make it out on that leg anyway, I don' think."

The pair had just come to an open glade, and in the pre-dawn fog Charlie could just make out the outline of two figures standing in plain sight on the far side of the clearing. That it was Harley Ponyboy and Thomas Begay was obvious. Under his breath Charlie mouthed, "What th…" *Are they idiots? Standing out in the open, not moving, surely they see us coming.* The two apparitions in the mist appeared to be unarmed; no sign of long arms, and a handgun would be useless at this distance.

The *mojado* looked perplexed. His own gun would be uncertain at this range. It was a trap of some sort, he was sure, but he would have to get within range to do anything about it. Luca nudged Charlie forward using the rifle barrel as a prod, staying close, using him as a shield as they moved forward. His nostrils flared as his every sense was brought to focus on this new danger. They were in the open now, and the *mojado* began chanting under his breath, repeating the same words over and over.

Charlie listened and was puzzled at what he took to be some native dialect from below the border—some *mestizo* prayer or appeal for good luck maybe. He knew the *mojado* was going to kill him; the only reason not to at this point was the need for a shield. When that was resolved, Charlie figured he would be the first to die, but by whose hand, he wasn't sure. He was certain his friends had a plan, but a plan by Harley and Thomas was far from a sure thing. He didn't even have the option of making a run for it. His knee felt like it might buckle at any moment.

The muzzle of the gun was hard against Charlie's spine, and a tingle went down his back as he edged forward. Fog swirled across the meadow, and he thought for a moment his rescuers would take advantage of it and do... *something*. The *mojado* looked past him—it was time to act. Charlie heard the click of the hammer being drawn and knew then his luck had run out.

A rifle boomed...but from a distance. Instantly, another shot blasted out, nearly behind him, this one the *mojado*'s. The bullet slammed harmlessly into the ground. Charlie whirled to see his captor staring blankly at the sky, his right hand pressing something to his breast as his legs folded under him. "*¿Me ves...?* Can you see me?" he asked in a calm voice.

Lurching sideways, Charlie's own knee gave way, and the two of them were face to face at arms' length. The *mojado*'s rifle lay in the mud, and as the man wavered, Charlie saw the broad blade of the knife in his left hand, and watched helplessly as the *mojado* drew back for a final deadly strike. The man jerked as once again the thunderclap of a rifle rolled across the meadow. The *mojado* cocked his head to the right—as though bitten on the neck by a hornet—the light faded from his eyes, and he smiled oddly at Charlie. His mouth moved and Charlie could barely discern the words before the man fell forward, face down in the mud...the clean red mud that reminded him so much of home.

A man in military camo strode toward Charlie from the woods and as he drew closer, Charlie could see it was Thomas's uncle, John Nez.

The ex-sniper approached, looked down at the figure on the ground, and then glanced at Charlie and said in a puzzled voice, "I never had to take two shots before." He scrutinized his rifle, a commercial version of the one he had carried in Vietnam. "Either I'm gett'n old... or he was one tough sonofabitch." He knelt and put a finger to the side of the *moja-do*'s neck, then, satisfied, asked, "What was he saying as he died?"

Charlie looked up and in a shaky voice said, "Oh, that… he asked me to tell his woman… that he had tried."

John Nez nodded, and waved for Thomas and Harley to come help.

# 20

## *Redemption*

Charlie Yazzie had long been of the opinion that no person was inherently evil—or good for that matter; rather that everyone was capable of either extreme, depending on the conditions brought to bear. It was a premise put forth by an early psych professor, and for the most part Charlie thought it to be true. In the case of Luca Tarango, however, he had a hard time justifying the notion. Later, when the ragged letter from the man's wife was found in his pocket, Charlie felt differently and thought it only right that he pass on her husband's last words. There would, of course, be official notification to next of kin, but only *he* knew what the man had said in his last moments. Charlie thought there might be value in that for the woman, but in the letter he sent, he didn't mention the circumstances of his death, only that his last thoughts had been of her. He didn't expect an answer... and he never got one, yet his mind was eased that he, too, at least had tried.

~~~~~~

Charlie's birthday fell not long after the Tarango case was officially closed, and at the small family get-together it still was a major topic of conversation.

Charlie Yazzie was generally given credit for ending the short reign of terror—though he vigorously denied it, assigning the bulk of the honor to Lieutenant Samuel Shorthair, who he maintained was the real hero of the affair... and to his two friends, Thomas Begay and Harley Ponyboy, who had persevered alongside him. He gave special praise to Thomas's Uncle John Nez, without whom he would no longer be among them he said—no one could argue with that. Charlie knew the ex-sniper and newly elected tribal councilman had not hesitated when his nephew secretly called him out to drive most of the night on bad reservation roads to arrive just before dawn.

When Thomas was asked why he had called on his uncle instead of notifying authorities, he said, "I knew my Uncle John would come without question, and he would do what had to be done to help us. Harley and me don't have much credit with the FBI—they likely wouldn't have helped us none. So I guess I just thought it best we handle it among our own people."

Charlie's Aunt, Annie Eagletree, still considered her nephew the hero, of course, and made sure everyone knew it. But to avoid being thought too prideful, she reported to all and sundry that her husband Clyde had been arrested and was in jail. Annie being true to her word was determined not to post bail for him. Even Clyde's aged mother had not stepped up, feeling his shenanigans reflected poorly on her status in the *billigaana* community, and this time at least he must pay the price.

Charlie's stock at Legal Services had gone up considerably. Some now thought he would be the one to take over when the "Old Man" stepped down, a thing not far distant in most people's opinion. And even Sue was impressed when FBI Agent Eldon Mayfield penned her husband a short missive of congratulations. Privately, however, Charlie thought he detected an undertone of disapproval, intimating a possible overstepping of bounds.

Harley Ponyboy was also proud of a letter delivered to Legal Services, but addressed to him. It was from his clan mother, "She Has Horses," and written for her by her nephew. "I just want to tell you, *shiye'ké*, that a heavy burden has been lifted from our hearts by the work you done to find the killer of our granddaughter. My sister and me send many prayers to your good." There was a short note at the end by the woman's nephew, stating he had written it exactly as his aunt wanted it... He said he would have done better had his aunt allowed it.

When shown the letter, Thomas said simply, "It was good of that old woman to write that." Thomas would long remember his time in the hands of the killer and knew they all still owed a great debt to his Uncle John Nez, and yet, he regretted not having a bigger part in the fugitive's demise.

~~~~~~~

Little did Charlie know that even as he enjoyed his birthday, there awaited a letter from his old college professor, George Custer, who, in the Navajo way, had come to be called the "little general," never in his presence, of course, but still that was how he was called.

None knew what changes that letter held... for all of them.

## ABOUT THE AUTHOR

Writer, poet R. Allen Chappell's work has appeared in magazines, literary and poetry publications, and has been featured on public radio and television. He grew up in New Mexico, at the edge of the great reservation.

Books in the Navajo Nation Mystery Series include.
*Navajo Autumn*
*Boy Made of Dawn*
*Ancient Blood*
*Mojado*
*Magpie Speaks*
*Wolves of Winter*

His unrelated short story collection *Fat of The Land* is also out on Amazon in both paperback and Kindle.

He and his wife spend most summers at home in western Colorado, where he pursues a lifelong interest in the pre-history of the region. He welcomes reader comments at:
rachappell@yahoo.com

If you've enjoyed this book, please consider going to its Amazon book page and leave a short review. It would be most appreciated.

Mojado

Glossary

1. *Acheii* — Grandfather *

2. *Athabaskan* — Navajo rootstock *

3. *Ashkii Ana'dlohi* — Laughing boy

4. *A-hah-la'nih* — affectionate greeting*

5. *Ah-wayh* — Baby

6. *Chindi* — (or chinde) Spirit of the dead *

7. *Dinè* — Navajo people

8. *Dinè Bikeyah* — Navajo country

9. *Hataalii* — Shaman (Singer)*

10. *Hastiin* — (Hosteen) Man or Mr. *

11. *Hogan* — (Hoogahn) dwelling or house

12. *Hozo* — To walk in beauty *

13. *Mojado* — Spanish for wet or soaked.*

14. *Shimásáni* — grandmother

15. *Shiye'ké* — My sons

16. *Tsé Bii' Ndzisgaii* — Monument Valley

17. *Yaa' eh t'eeh* — Greeting; Hello

18. *Yeenaaldiooshii* — Skinwalker; witch*

19. *billigaana* — white people

See Notes

Mojado

## Notes

1. *Acheii* — Grandfather – there are several words for Grandfather depending on how formal the intent and the gender of the speaker.

2. *Athabaskan* — The Northern Paleo-Indian ancestors, of the Navajo and Apache. Sometimes referred to as Athabasca or even Athapaskans.

4. *A-hah-la'nih* — A greeting - affectionate version of Yaa eh t'eeh, generally only used among family and close friends.

6. *Chindi* – When a person dies inside a hogan, it is said that his chindi or spirit remains there forever, causing the hogan to be abandoned. Chindi are not considered benevolent entities. For the traditional Navajo, just speaking a dead person's name may call up his chindi and cause harm to the speaker or others.

9. *Hataalii* – Generally known as a "Singer" among the Dinè, these men are considered "Holy Men" and have apprenticed to older practitioners—sometimes for many years—to learn the ceremonies. They make the sand paintings that are an integral part of the healing and know the many songs that must be sung in the correct order.

10. *Hastiin* — Literal translation is "man" but is often considered the word for "Mr." as well. Hosteen is the usual Anglo version.

12. *Hozo* – For the Navajo "hozo" (sometimes hozoji) is a general state of well-being, both physical and spiritual, that indicates a certain "state of grace," which is referred to as "walking in beauty." Illness or depression, is the usual cause of "loss of hozo," which puts one out of sync with the people as a whole. There are ceremonies to restore hozo and return the ailing person to a oneness with his people.

13. *Mojado* — Spanish for wet or soaked. In the Southwest it is a common euphemism for wetback or illegal immigrant.

14. *Shih-chai* — Father. There are several words for Father depending on the degree of formality intended and sometimes even the gender of the speaker.

21. *Yeenaaldiooshii* – These witches, as they are often referred to, are the chief source of evil or fear in the traditional Navajo superstitions. They are thought to be capable of many unnatural acts, such as flying, or turning themselves into werewolves and other ethereal creatures; hence the term Skinwalkers, referring to their ability to change forms or skins.